Arias of Blood

Also by John Gano

Death at the Opera

Inspector Proby's Christmas
Inspector Proby in Court
Inspector Proby's Weekend

John Gano

Arias of Blood

St. Martin's Press ❧ New York

M

Library of Congress Cataloging-in-Publication Data

Gano, John.
     Arias of blood / John Gano.
          p.   cm.
     ISBN 0-312-16775-X
     I. Title.
PR6057.A47A89   1997
823'.914—dc21   97-16503
                                             CIP

First published in Great Britain by Macmillan, an imprint of Macmillan Publishers Ltd

First U.S. Edition: October 1997

10   9   8   7   6   5   4   3   2   1

Historical Note:

'On the morning of April 22nd, when news of the Duke of Cumberland's victory at Culloden Field reached London, a posse of militia headed by the Earl of Greenwich surrounded the Mansion House. They demanded entry to arrest the Lord Mayor, Sir Wilbraham Smith, on a warrant issued by the Chief Justice on suspicion of aiding the Jacobites.

On being granted access by the City Serjeant, they could find no trace of the miscreant, though they searched the place most diligently for upwards of eleven days.'

A New History of the '45
Benedict Noel
(Cooper & Hay)
p.373

THE
FLORIA TOSCA
Grand Opera Company

present

La Traviata

Opera in three Acts by Giuseppe Verdi
Libretto by Francesco Maria Piave

Cast:

Violetta, a courtesan	Isabelle Morny
Alfredo, her admirer	Gerard Combe
Germont, his father	Winston Wheeler
Baron Douphol	Bruno Retz
Annina, her maid	Jane Nuneham
Flora, her friend	Maria Cellini
Doctor Grenvil	Edmund Nuneham
Visconte Gastone	Rupert Brock
Marchese d'Obigny	Henry Timpson
Director of Music	George Sinclair
Producer & Wardrobe	Jane Nuneham
Stage Manager	Edmund Nuneham

*We gratefully acknowledge the
assistance of Schumann & Goldwater plc,
in sponsoring tonight's performance*

Arias of Blood

Chapter One

'A *quell'amor, quell'amo-or ch'è palpito!*' The pure sound of Kiri Te Kanawa's honeyed soprano filled the tall room, with its heavy portraits and thick-fringed velvet curtains that hid the view over London's Eaton Square.

Sir Peter Hopkirk looked up angrily at the distraction of the door to his study opening. It was the first time in the seven weeks he had been under Special Branch protection that anyone had entered without knocking first.

But if that was a surprise, it was as nothing to what followed. For there, walking with a confident smile across the thick carpet towards him, was *himself*. For someone who had spent many pleasurable hours in front of a mirror, tweaking his luxuriant red beard, it was an unexpectedly weird sensation.

'Is this some kind of joke?' he snapped, angry to find that his hand was shaking.

1

The other Sir Peter shook his head, still smiling. 'Not really,' he said. 'Not now.'

'Are you meant to take my place?'

'In a way.' The man could even copy his voice cadences!

'It's very convincing.' He tried to match the other's smile, but was conscious of a miserable rictus disfiguring his face. 'Who are you when you're not me?'

'I?' said the other, standing now directly in front of him. 'I am *Death*.' And he drove the stiletto he had concealed behind his hand deep into the businessman's throat, twisting it so viciously that only a momentary gurgle betrayed the violence inside that sumptuous room.

' . . . *croce e delizia, delizia al cor! Ah-ah-ah-ahhh!*' On sang the diva, mechanically oblivious to the discordant scene, her radiant voice echoing stereophonically from the four speakers placed around on top of the fitted mahogany bookshelves.

Pausing only to drag the still palpitating body of his victim behind the further sofa, the other Sir Peter sat down at the broad desk and calmly pressed the button beside his telephone. Immediately he heard footsteps on the marble floor outside, followed by a discreet knock.

'Come in!'

'Yes, Sir Peter?' It was a young man, already bald, with thick spectacles and a nervous air.

2

'Tell Denny I'd like the car brought round in five minutes.'

'You're going out, Sir Peter?' The young man sounded shocked.

'Why not? The bloodhounds can follow, can't they? I've had enough of skulking in here today. Place smells like a morgue!' Indeed it did, and he had suddenly noticed a cloying wetness on his sleeve where stray blood must have spurted. 'Tell the Chief Inspector I'm going to Threadneedle Street.'

'Are you sure . . . ?' The young man was hesitating.

'Just do it, if you please!' It helped that the real Sir Peter was known to be impatient and irascible.

As soon as the door closed behind the abject secretary, he crossed quickly to the big gilded mirror over the mantelpiece to check his appearance. There was no blood on his shirt and his beard was really quite becoming. He gave it an affectionate tweak. Back at the desk, he extracted a long cigar from the silver casket there and lit it. Anything to smother the reek of blood. He coughed and wiped his eyes hurriedly, crossing to the mirror a second time to check his face.

Another knock. 'Yes?'

'The car is here.' Just a frightened face round the door. What did Sir Peter *do* to his staff, to make them all so subservient?

He strode into the hall and allowed the young

man to help him into a heavy cashmere coat. 'Thank you, Gervase.'

'Thank *you*, Sir Peter.'

'I really must protest!' A fat man was hurrying down the stairs, wiping his mouth.

The new Sir Peter laughed. 'I hope I haven't interrupted your dinner, Chief Inspector. Don't come too near! I've caught this damned flu.' He pulled out a voluminous handkerchief and blew his nose loudly, conveniently obscuring his upper face in the process. It was mid-November, and even in this big stone house tiny currents of wintry air wound their way here and there through the overheated rooms.

'The warnings were quite specific.'

'I have to see the Deputy Governor about Klein-worts. The whole business of the City can't grind to a halt because of a few cranks.' He blew a dense cloud of cigar smoke into the policeman's face.

'This man has killed before.'

'So you say. Now. I think you're in my way.' The big policeman stepped obediently aside. 'I've no doubt you'll be following me?'

'Of course. And DS Smithers will ride with you.'

'No, thank you,' said the new Sir Peter, already half out of the door. 'I need to do some discreet telephoning. But I'll tell Denny to drive slowly. That way your driver can keep up. Unlike this morning.' He slammed the door.

The policeman shook his head. 'What a bastard!'

The secretary smirked. 'He never changes.' And went back across the hall to his lonely tray of sand- wiches in front of his office computer.

Twenty minutes passed in peaceful, uninter- rupted work. Then suddenly the telephone rang.

'Yes? Denny?' There was incoherent shouting the other end. *'Disappeared?'* He could hardly make out the chauffeur's garbled words. 'At the traffic lights? I don't understand. Can't you speak slower?'

Still the voice clamoured on. He sighed. 'You'd better wait there,' he said, seizing on a pause. 'I'm sure it's a misunderstanding.' And replaced the receiver. He peered at the screen. The dollar was rising sharply. And someone was selling Swiss francs again. He stood up, stretched and walked slowly back across the hall and into his master's study. There was no need to knock, since he knew the room was empty.

He wrinkled his nose. The air was filthy. It smelt like . . . he crossed to the fire and stumbled. There, lying half hidden behind the sofa, was, unmistak- ably, the reeking blood-soaked body of his employer.

Chapter Two

'Financier Found Butchered!'

shrieked the Sunday headline;

'Threatened tycoon stabbed in Study!'

'More *tisane?*'

'I'd rather have a gin and tonic.' George Sinclair, pianist, impresario, vocal coach and whatever else might pay the rent of a two-room basement flat in Shepherd's Bush, put down the newspaper with some reluctance.

'It's eleven o'clock in the morning!'

'All right. A glass of wine then.'

'Get it yourself, *chéri.*' The blonde woman beside him curled herself down under the bedclothes and closed her eyes. 'I'm sleepy.'

'Where were you last night?'

She ignored him, so he turned back to the paper.

T HE body of Sir Peter Hopkirk, multimillion-aire Chief Executive of the international conglomerate Badison Group, was found stabbed to death in his house in Eaton Square last night. Sir Peter had been under armed guard since receiving a series of written threats from 'Solomon', the pseudonym of a terrorist believed to have been responsible for the deaths of major financial figures in Frankfurt and New York.

Scotland Yard issued a brief statement at 10 p.m. last night confirming that Sir Peter had been murdered and saying that the police were following a number of leads. His secretary Gervase Jacobs found the body and there is speculation that the threats had been linked to Badison Group's antici- pated takeover of the ailing City insurance giant Dupont Assurance.

(*see Financial Section page 32*)

'So, *mon ange*. What is so interesting?' She had emerged again.

'Where were you last night?'

'Having fun.' She pouted. 'We never go out any more. Where is the fun in staying home and singing scales? I am younger than you. I need a little *gaiété* in my life. I gave up my apartment to share with you, but to share what?'

He shrugged, more depressed than angry. 'I know,' he said sadly, 'but we have no money. I'd love to take you to The Dancing Dervish. But with whisky at thirty pounds a glass . . . '

'Alasdair asked you, too.'

'Very insincerely.'

It was her turn to shrug. 'Who cares if it's sincere, if he's buying your whisky drink at thirty pounds a glass?'

'I care!' His sallow face had suddenly flushed.

'He's a sir.'

'What's that mean?'

'It means he's *Sir* Rumbold. Except he doesn't use it.'

'I'm not surprised!'

She stared at him. 'Jane said you used to look like the young Byron. Today I should say you looked like the old Balzac.'

'Jane said you looked like a tart in that leopard-skin outfit,' he countered.

She laughed. 'She should know, I suppose.' He smiled and turned to the back pages. 'It's ages since we made love,' she added slyly.

He put the paper down with an angry rustle. 'You know we can't,' he said. 'I'm your brother, in case you'd forgotten.'

She shrugged her shoulders, deliberately allowing one strap of her negligée to slip, thus revealing one deliciously pink nipple. 'It is sex we make not babies. It is normal to need the feel of a man, even in England?'

'Not if he's your brother. I suppose they have laws about that even in France?' He glowered into the middle distance, carefully ignoring the nipple. 'It was different before we *knew*. Anyway, it doesn't make me feel very sexy, knowing you've been out all night with *Sir* Alasdair Rumbold, of all people.'

'What's wrong with Alasdair Rumbold then?'

'He's seven feet high, has hair on his nose and he's *rich*.'

She giggled. 'He's got hair on his back too!'

'How do you know?' This time he sounded seriously angry.

'Because he took all his clothes off in the car.'

'He did *what?*'

She laughed delightedly. 'I love it when you're jealous, *Georges*. It was very amusing. I grabbed the steering wheel and kept my hand on the horn until all these people came . . . '

'And . . . ?' He was watching her carefully.

'And then I got out and thanked him for a lovely evening. Everyone thought it was very funny.'

'Even Alasdair?'

She shook her head. 'Perhaps not.'

'You're not *still* reading that journal?' She was framed in the bathroom doorway, lithe and blonde as a Botticelli Venus, with the light painting soft shadows across her naked belly.

He caught his breath and put it down. 'It's interesting,' he said, and swallowed painfully.

'What is it about?'

'It's about an anonymous madman who goes round murdering businessmen.'

'Alasdair's a businessman,' she said thoughtfully.

'I take it all back! The man's a public servant.'

She giggled. 'And he likes opera.'

George paused. 'Alasdair? How much?'

'*Much* more now he knows I sing.'

'Enough to book us?'

She arched over him, so that her breasts brushed his face. 'He'd give *anything* to be in your shoes.'

'No doubt.' He could feel the familiar pain of jealousy throbbing in his chest, an ache that seemed to invade him now with increasing persistence, just as his body ached rebelliously for hers. His sister! And to find out after so many nights of love. And now it had been five, no, six long months since they had made love, yet they still slept in the same bed. Like brother and sister. 'But would he give five thousand to see you sing ... what ... *Despina?*'

'*Despina!*' She snorted angrily. 'My voice is growing. I'm not a soubrette any longer. I can sing big parts.'

'Name one.' He was back in the newspaper, riffling through the pages to find the financial reports.

'*Violetta.*'

'This is interesting,' he said. 'Porters' have made

10

one hundred and thirty-two million pre-tax. The shares are up fourteen pence.' She sighed and turned away. 'Where are you off to now?'

'I'm going to practise.'

'Why have you got your grumpy-French-tart face on?'

'Why don't you *fuck* yourself, *con*!' She slammed the door so hard that two of his photograph frames fell off the dresser. Reluctantly putting down the paper, he stooped to pick them up. One was of his mother, a thin tired woman who had once sung in a production of *Rosenkavalier* conducted by his father. The other was of Isabelle sitting on his lap, both of them laughing, in Florian's in Venice the previous autumn. It all seemed a very long time ago. With an angry shrug, he turned back to the newspaper.

Chapter Three

'I still don't see how he had time to get back to the house.' An uncomfortable Detective Chief Inspector Lowe was in conference with his Commander, Stephen Bright, and, beside him across the table on the left, the Assistant Commissioner (Homicide), Sebastian Moseley-Morgan. They had been at it for three hours, and Lowe wasn't at all sure that he still had a career to look forward to.

Commander Bright lit another cigarette and leant forward in his chair, tapping his pen on the desk, a ragged tattoo with no discernible rhythm. A thin toothy terrier of a man with sparse white hair and close-set pale blue eyes, he gave off a constant air of nervous rage, which did nothing to reassure the portly chief inspector.

Moseley-Morgan, by contrast, short and chubby, had a pink moon face and a relaxed, almost paternal, air with one exception. His smiles never reached his eyes, which, pale grey and reptilian, gazed out with chilling indifference on all the imperfections of the world about him. There was one other oddity about him. An encounter with wire stretched by terrorists across a road in Ulster had left him with just a whisper for a voice.

Now he was smiling at the Chief Inspector. 'Remind me,' he breathed, 'of the timings involved. Sir Peter left the house at . . . '

The Chief Inspector consulted his notes yet again. Sweat was pouring down inside his shirt, but he didn't dare glance to see if it showed through his jacket. '19.23,' he read. They must have been through this seventeen times or more. Bright made a note.

'You followed in the Rover?'

'Yes, sir.' More scratching from the Commander's pen.

'And you didn't spot Sir Peter leaving the car at any time before you reached the Bank of England?'

'No, sir.'

'At 20.01?'

He risked a frantic look at his own notes. He'd been word-perfect when he'd come in. Now he could barely swear to his own name. 'Yes. 20.01.'

'The chauffeur thought he heard something at the second set of traffic lights on the Embankment?' Commander Bright suddenly rasped into the conversation, his voice unnaturally loud after the Assistant Commissioner's dull croak.

'By Blackfriars, yes.' The Chief Inspector nodded enthusiastically. 'That's what he said.'

'So why didn't you see anything?' Again the dreadful whisper from his left. 'Tell us that. If you would.'

'Perhaps there was nothing to see.' The poor man was thrashing about in rising panic. They knew all this. Because he'd told them the same thing. Over and over again. 'Perhaps he got out at the first lights.'

'Or the third?' put in Bright sarcastically. 'Or the nineteenth?'

'No, sir.' The Chief Inspector shook his head with stolid certainty. 'There are only three sets of lights on the Embankment there. Both cars turned off to go up Queen Victoria Street.'

The two senior officers looked at each other. Bright sighed. 'The secretary found the body at 20.04, after the chauffeur alerted him. The log shows you passed Blackfriars at 19.53. There's no way he could have got back to Eaton Square in that time, dead or alive. What's more, according to the chauffeur, those lights were the first you stopped at. Which means . . . '

'Which means,' croaked Moseley-Morgan with a ghastly smile, 'that Sir Peter Hopkirk never got into the car at all. *He was already dead when you came downstairs.*'

'But . . . ' Lowe wiped his forehead again and again in his agitation. 'I *talked* to him. He wasn't dead when I talked to him.'

'The man you bloody talked to,' shouted the Commander, 'was *Solomon*.' And he dug his pen into his notebook so hard that it snapped off. 'You were close enough to arrest him there and then! You'd spent nearly two months with Sir Peter. Surely you could tell the two men apart?'

'He had flu.' Lowe was suddenly concentrating hard. 'He told me not to come too close. And he was smoking one of those stinking cigars. I thought it was odd at the time.'

'Now he tells us,' whispered Moseley-Morgan, still with the same unconvincing smile. 'Still, I think we have the full picture now. You can leave us, Lowe.'

The big man stood up thankfully and walked as fast as he could towards the door. 'Oh, Lowe!' It was the Commander who called after him.

'Yes, sir?'

'Today's Sunday. Take tomorrow off and then report to Traffic Statistics Tuesday morning. You'll be based in Ongar. Good morning.'

'What now?' The two men, left alone, stared at each other in silent despair. 'He's killed three so far, and not a hint of a clue.'

'Nothing from Forensic?' whispered the Assistant Commissioner, turning his head methodically first to the right and then to the left, but slowly, as his physiotherapist had advised.

'Not yet. They're not hopeful. Death between seven and eight, not instantaneous but pretty quick. He'd severed his windpipe and his vocal cords—'

'I know the feeling.'

Bright looked away to hide his sudden embarrassment. 'He used something small but sharp, with a serrated edge.'

'Nasty!'

'It's odd,' mused Bright. 'He shot von Arnim and hanged Dwight Tait, whose body was in a dreadful state. There seems to be no common currency.'

'Other than announcing the sentence in advance, though without giving us the motive.'

Bright laughed. 'Well, he can't do that. Otherwise we'd know who he was.'

'It is a he, I suppose.'

'Can you see a woman impersonating Sir Peter Hopkirk? No, at least we've narrowed the field by fifty per cent. Who's next, do you suppose?'

'I'm sure Solomon will tell us when he's ready. What's the name of the man Interpol are sending?'

'Dumeige. Paul Dumeige.'

Chapter Four

In the heart of the City of London, at a busy intersection formed by no fewer than six major roads, and perched awkwardly athwart the stanchions of the Bank underground railway station stands the Mansion House, hub of the City's social life and home (for his one year of office only) to the incumbent Lord Mayor of London.

Built in the early 1740s by the architect George Dance, this, his masterpiece, towers up four storeys of super-confident Baroquerie. Wrap-round Corinthian pilasters, deeply carved rustications and thickly sliced architraves all testify to the wealth and sheer chutzpah of the City Fathers in the time of the Georges. It survived the London Blitz and the latest and best efforts of Hitler's flying bombs only to risk succumbing to the missionary zeal of the postwar developers. Saved (only just) by a determined campaign by the newly formed Georgian Group, it forms the principal focus in a matchless group of municipal buildings which include the

Bank of England, the Royal Exchange and St Mary Woolnoth.

Two weeks before had seen the triumphant procession of the Lord Mayor's Show marking the assumption of office of Mr Alderman Reginald Threlfall, partner in the leading City stockbrokers of Sterling, Gadsby and Chown, non-executive director of both Commercial Union and the Midland Bank, and, for the past two years, a Director of the Royal Opera House, Covent Garden. While the ground floor of the Mansion House is largely occupied by domestic offices, and the first floor by the grand ceremonial rooms, the second floor is the domain of the Lord Mayor and his family.

This last comprises on the west (Walbrook) side the Dining Room and its associated Morning Room for the reception of the private guests, on the north side a broad blue hallway, panelled in wood known as the Blue Corridor, and beyond that the tall cream stuccoed Ballroom leading to the three State guest rooms, and on the east side the Boudoir, used as the family's private drawing room and beyond that the Lord Mayor's Bedroom. The whole of the south side is taken up with the upper storey of the immense Egyptian Hall, entered from the floor below but rising a titanic fifty-seven feet to the tip of its gold coffered ceiling.

However, between the inner wall of the Egyptian Hall and that of the inner central court lies a long thin chamber, toplit by an ornamental cupola. Sometimes this has been used as the Lord Mayor's dressing room (when relations between the great man and his wife have been less than cosy), and sometimes just as a convenient corridor leading from the Bedroom (east) to the Dining Room (west).

Under the new regime of Mr Alderman Reginald Threlfall, the doors at either end had been strengthened and new keys of an intricate design fitted, and it had then been given over entirely to a mass of filing cabinets, two heavy desks and a bank of computer screens. Only one man, his long-time assistant Jerry, had the set of three keys needed to enter this stronghold, and the state of the Threlfalls' marriage could be gauged by the fact that Mrs Alderman Reginald Threlfall, the new Lady Mayoress, had been allotted (and had accepted) the smallest of the State guest rooms reached by crossing the Ballroom.

Certainly she was never granted access to the narrow chamber where her husband spent as much of the day as his ceremonial duties would allow.

'You're sure these computers are secure?'

'Of course, *my Lord Mayor.*' Jerry just managed to suppress a snigger as he used his employer's new official mode of address.

Threlfall, heavy-boned and bulky, with a large nose and thick matted grey brows, turned angrily on his hunched assistant. 'Don't start that again,' he snapped. 'The joke's wearing thin.'

Jerry, younger, slighter, very bent, scratched his scrawny neck. 'It's no joke. My life's difficult enough here as it is. It's what they expect me to call you. You can't be Reggie one minute and *My Lord Mayor* the next. I've got enough to worry about with this new Serious Fraud Office team on our backs.'

The First Gentleman of the City shrugged his shoulders. 'How close are they?'

'Miles adrift! But I'll tell you what.'

'What?'

'I think they might be getting close to the Royal Barbican Banking Corporation.'

Threlfall chuckled. 'I can't think how that lot've got away with it for so long. Crooks every last one of them!'

His assistant nodded. 'But one of the SFO young women was round asking questions in Barclays' head office.'

'About what?' asked the Lord Mayor scornfully.

'Your land purchases.'

Threlfall's smile died away. 'About Redwood Park?'

'Exactly.'

'*Bastards!*'

His assistant's voice dropped lower. 'What if they pick up on the money used?'

Threlfall shook his head. 'We've got Her Majesty's Judges dining here *en masse* next Thursday night. I'll have a quiet word with the DPP.'

'Be careful!' Jerry's face had lengthened. 'That might backfire.'

'Not when you remember what we've got in File 53.'

Jerry's eyes widened. 'The *DPP*?'

'Look it up.' A white telephone beside Threlfall's chair let out a dull buzz. 'Yes? No! I told you I didn't want to be disturbed. Least of all by the Press. What is my Private Secretary for if not this. I don't care what they say. Ask Brigadier Gooch to handle it.' He slammed down the receiver.

'Did you say File 53?' asked Jerry in an odd voice.

'Yes,' snapped his angry employer. 'Why do you ask?'

'There's nothing in it.' The little man was tapping anxiously at fresh keys on his computer keyboard.

'Bloody nonsense! It's got all the juicy bits.'

'See for yourself! There's just one item.'

Threlfall heaved his swollen body out of the chair and lumbered over to the other screen. He stared at the single sentence, and reached out a shaky hand to steady himself. There flickering on the green fascia, in minuscule letters, was the simple message:

I, Solomon, sentence you to death within one week. Prepare yourself!

Chapter Five

In the uncertain twilit world of the Floria Tosca Grand Opera Company, darkness was more regular than light. Two years ago they, that is George, had been employed to give only two performances, of *Così Fan Tutte*. Last year, by contrast, had seen plans for ten *Don Giovannis* (due to a rival's collapse) expand miraculously to twelve thanks to considerable publicity arising from a murder case. This year seemed likely to close without a single engagement, none of his previous employers having been willing to consider a return visit.

It was a source of some chagrin to George that other more expensive companies seemed able to make a living, however precarious, on the stately home circuit, while he seemed doomed to spend the rest of his life playing for *thés dansants* at the Esplanade Hotel, Seaford, all summer, and accompanying the beautiful Isabelle at auditions, and the occasional *soirée*, all winter.

But suddenly, light had returned. Coming in wet

and cold from a fruitless application for work as *répétiteur* at Sadler's Wells, he had found his answer-machine returned to life with a winking red signal. A message! He pressed the button and waited impatiently while the machine shook itself, vibrated for several minutes to no obvious purpose, and finally disgorged its news: *'Hello! Hello! Oh dear, it's one of those dreadful answer-things. Do you think they can hear me? This is . . . um . . . Janet Tabley calling from Cheshire, my number is . . . oh God! they will keep changing it . . . it's, can you remember, darling? . . . I think it's . . . '* There was a loud *pee-eep* and the machine switched itself off.

He pulled off his sodden overcoat and went to pour himself a necessary glass of vodka when the telephone rang again.

'Hello?'

'Is that you?'

'George Sinclair here.'

'Oh thank God! I was afraid you were that machine again.'

'Mrs Tabley?'

A pause. *'Lady*, actually.' He frowned. 'I mean, Lady Tabley, if you see what I mean.' She laughed painfully.

Business! An employer! 'Yes, hello, Lady Tabley,' he said, trying to infuse some sincere geniality into a voice that was crying out for the vodka bottle, just out of reach on the far table.

'Hello. You do operas? Isn't that right?'

'I certainly do.' In his current state of solvency, he'd do Punch and Judy shows if anyone would pay him.

'Are you *dreadfully* expensive?'

He smiled a thin slick smile to himself. 'I don't think this is a market where you want a cheap failure,' he said, and paused.

She gasped. 'Oh *God* no! Certainly not!'

'Well, quality always has its price, wouldn't you agree?' What did the Tableys *do*, for God's sake? Groceries, Gatling guns or just plain *sex* with one of the grosser monarchs? There was no way of guessing from her strangulated bleat. 'We prefer to make sure of making your evening a success. Is it for charity or a family party?' One of the Honourable Little Tableys' coming-out perhaps or the anniversary of Lord Tabley's release on licence?

'It's for those darling lifeboatmen, actually. So brave, don't you think?'

'Absolute heroes,' he said. This sort of thing was catching. 'Men of *oak*!'

'I'm sorry?'

Had he overdone it? 'Which opera would you like?'

She giggled. 'You mean I can *choose*. Darling!' She was talking almost inaudibly to someone in the background, 'He says I can choose which opera. Well, who do you think? The opera man! What? Yes, of course I've asked how much.' Her voice became louder again. 'My husband wants to know how much.'

'That,' said George smoothly, 'depends on the opera. Our bargain basement special introductory offer is *Così Fan Tutte* at . . . ' he thought quickly, not unheedful of that morning's sheaf of brown envelopes, ' . . . five thousand pounds.' She remained splendidly silent. No audible intakes of breath or hysterical little shriekettes. 'Or we could do this year's special offer, *La Traviata*, newly costumed, for seven thousand pounds.'

'Eek!'

'Excuse me?' Had she really said '*eek*'?

There was whispering in the background. 'My husband says what about *Riggo*-something-or-other. Apparently they did it at Brooks' the other night and some very pretty girl got knifed, and everyone stood up and cheered.'

'*Rigoletto*,' said George through gritted teeth. The company concerned had tried to poach Isabelle, and she was still thinking about it. 'That would be very expensive, I'm afraid.'

More off-stage muttering. 'My husband says why?'

George thought hard. 'Because it needs a big chorus, and two pianists. We'd be *absolutely delighted* to do it for you, but the price. . . . '

'It's okay!' she said suddenly. 'Prosper says *Traviata* will do fine. Seven thousand pounds?'

'Plus VAT,' put in George, with heaven-sent inspiration. 'I'm sure you can claim it back.'

'Goodness you are clever,' said Lady Tabley. 'What happens now?'

'I send you a contract, you send me a cheque for fifty per cent up front, and I start rehearsing.'

She gave another girlish giggle. 'You make it sound fearfully easy!'

'That's my job,' said George. 'When do you want the show?'

'When? Oh, didn't I say? Next Saturday.'

'*Next Saturday?*'

'Yes. We were having Opera-Made-Easy, but they've collapsed or something funny. So someone Prosper knew said they thought you weren't very busy at the moment. We've sold all the tickets. Over twenty thousand pounds, can you imagine that?'

George could. 'Where's the show?'

'Didn't I say? It's at the Mansion House.'

He frowned. 'Which one?'

There was a lot of girlish laughter tinkling down the line, and he had to listen to his question being repeated not once, but twice, for Prosper, Lord Tabley, and his pals or whoever. 'There's only one Mansion House,' she said at last. 'In the *City*.' He couldn't face asking which city, so rang off after getting her London address for sending the contract: 127, The Vale, London S.W.3. He had a job. He had six days. Now all he needed were some singers.

Chapter Six

'One week. That's the shortest timescale he's set himself so far.'

'You think it's a game to him, don't you?'

'Yes, *Commandeur*. I do.' The young man sitting across the desk from Commander Bright on Monday morning was in his early thirties, tall, erect and with an almost perfect profile beneath glossy black hair just long enough to suggest a continental hairdresser. The sole imperfection in the profile was that his nose bore some evidence of having been recently broken.

Bright fixed his enquiring gaze upon it. 'Those Neapolitan terrorists?'

'My nose?' The man called Paul Dumeige laughed. 'No, indeed. A young lady in the Bois de Boulogne. What style! A tigress . . . ' he laughed in open exultation. ' . . . with attitude.'

The Commander stared at him for a moment. Such an incident in England would give rise to half a year's work for Internal Affairs. Whereas Interpol. . . . ! He shrugged. 'Are you armed?'

The young man inclined his head without speaking, then gravely put a finger to his lips. 'Least said soonest mended. Is that not one of your proverbs?'

Those who knew the Commander would have recognized in his answering smile the signs of trouble. The man from Interpol saw nothing, but that was perhaps his deliberate choice. 'My own men have to operate under the strictest rules,' Bright said, in a clipped tone.

'I understand.' Dumeige had no wish to alienate the older man. On the contrary, the success of his mission depended on close co-operation between all parties. 'Now, about the latest target?'

Bright clasped his hands together. 'The Lord Mayor? Unprecedented! Reginald Threlfall is one of the pillars of the City. String of directorships, highly respected stockbroker, a man of great distinction.'

'You have nothing against him?' A feline question, delicately put.

'In what way?' The Commander was not above a little felinity on his own account.

'Well . . . ' Dumeige opened his hands in Gallic speculation. 'No rumours, no whispers . . . ?' His blue eyes were fixed firmly on the little Commander, whose own gaze wavered.

'I suspect you of being very well briefed,' said

Bright sourly. Another Gallic gesture of genial agreement confirmed his surmise. 'So! There is some doubt. An unconfirmed leak here, an unreliable accusation there. His name has come up once or twice in unexpected contexts. . . . ' His voice trailed away. How much did the bloody Frog know?

Dumeige, as if reading his mind, smiled. 'The Serious Fraud Office are investigating him, perhaps?'

Bright opened his lips in what looked close to a sneer. 'Yes,' he said.

'With a South Italian connection?'

'That's what my opposite number surmises.'

'Yet the man is your Lord Mayor?'

Bright shrugged. 'It's different from your French mayors. The man has no executive function.'

'He sits as a judge.'

'A magistrate,' corrected Bright. 'Very minor cases.'

It was Dumeige who shrugged now. 'It is curious, even so. When can we meet him?'

Bright rose to his feet. 'The car is waiting for us now.'

There are, officially, only two ways into the Mansion House: either by the main hall door on Walbrook, presided over by the Porter, Ted, or by the staff door under the front pediment and immediately opposite the Bank of England. Here the security guards, under the operational control of the Sword-Bearer, Colonel Lumsden, vet all who enter and leave, entering their names and business in the heavy Morocco-bound Daily Journal. Even in the nineteenth century there was considerable security needed because of the sheer weight of bullion used in the City's collection of gold and silver plate.

But since Lord Samuel of High Cross bequeathed his very extensive collection of Dutch paintings to be hung there, a collection valued conservatively at over thirty million pounds, the perceived need for active security has doubled.

There are also two official emergency exits, both on the southern side of the building abutting a narrow pedestrian alley leading from Walbrook into Mansion House Place. The first is via a barred and alarmed metal door leading directly into the main kitchens; the second is from a specially adapted window at the rear of the first floor Egyptian Hall on to a swinging metal fire escape.

Finally there is also a fifth, unofficial, secret means of access through an armoured door in the basement at the back of the old police cells which leads, via a short tunnel, into the reinforced concrete police bunker beneath the Bank station booking office. This, a relic of the nuclear emergency planning in the Fifties, serves as a strategic command post for anti-terrorist protection of the Square Mile, and as such would not welcome regular passers-by, not even Lord Mayors. Indeed the only member of the Mansion House staff to have the access codes of this door is the Sword-Bearer, a post traditionally reserved for retired senior officers of, or previously attached to, the Intelligence Corps, and currently held by Lieutenant-Colonel Bruce Lumsden.

Commander Bright and Paul Dumeige chose the main Walbrook door, ringing the ornate gold bell and waiting patiently while the video camera recorded their faces for Colonel Lumsden's nightly security review.

'Welcome, gents!' Ted, the Porter, had once been one of the upstairs footmen, but a catholic taste for the variety of bottles on offer had made his serving at meals too risky, hence his promotion and hence also his ripe complexion and fruity vowels. He liked Monday afternoons, indeed any afternoons. They set him humming, since they meant that the evening, a period for prolonged self-indulgence, was only just around the corner. 'The Brigadier is through there. He will take you up to the Lord Mayor.'

Passing through a low but richly carved arch, they were ushered up wide blue-carpeted stairs by a stout man with a very large and glossy black moustache who introduced himself as the Lord Mayor's Private Secretary, Brigadier Gooch. They followed this stately guide through a lobby, turning left by a fine statue of Apollo, and then into a light airy room overlooking the busy junction outside. Unexpectedly, there was background music, a woman singing something operatic. The volume, apparently operated from outside the room, discreetly died away to silence.

'Gentlemen! Thank you for coming.' Threlfall came round the desk and shook hands solemnly with both men. 'I'm sorry to be the cause of disrupting what I'm sure must be very busy schedules.'

Bright murmured politely while Paul Dumeige studied their host with interest. Five foot ten, he reckoned, and over seventeen stone, or more. The Lord Mayor might once have been a handsome man, but the swelling of his flesh had so smudged his features that they now stood out individually, thick red lips, a heavy porous nose, sagging bloodshot cheeks, a chin within a chin, within indeed a further chin, rather than reading as a face. Clearly he could afford an excellent tailor, since his torso, though very large, gave the impression of extreme smartness, and his shoes, poking out at them through the knee-hole of the desk, shone with a military gloss.

As if suddenly aware of the scrutiny, Threlfall turned to the Frenchman and offered him a box of cigars. 'Romeos?'

Dumeige shook his head. 'No, thank you.'

Threlfall stared at him for a moment. 'Have we met before?'

The other man smiled slightly. 'Not that I can recall,' he said. 'Now, about Solomon . . . '

The Lord Mayor laughed. 'Bloody nonsense! It's typical of the tabloid press.'

'You didn't sound overly surprised when my office rang you this morning,' said Bright cautiously.

Threlfall shrugged. 'In the modern business world empty threats are not unknown.'

'Yet Solomon's letter to the editor of the *Sun* had not been published at that point.'

Threlfall's hesitation was only fractional. 'My dear . . . er . . . Commander! I'd had three calls from enterprising journalists before your people rang. I knew very well that I was being threatened.'

Bright sat back in the chair he had selected beside the Mayoral desk. 'That's all right then,' he said. 'I had wondered whether Solomon had been in touch direct.'

Threlfall shook his head, and his eyes again shifted to examine the Frenchman standing in profile by the window. "Fraid not. Perhaps he doesn't know my address!' He chuckled.

Dumeige turned back from the window. 'A famous view!'

'The Bank of England?'

'One of the world's great institutions.'

'Tell me,' interrupted Bright impatiently, 'does the name Solomon mean anything to you?'

Threlfall selected a cigar himself, and very carefully bit the end off. 'No,' he said, and, putting the cigar into his mouth, he struck a match and applied its flame. A column of aromatic blue smoke ascended towards the high ceiling with its deeply carved stucco panels. 'It means nothing to me.'

'Apart from what you've read,' put in the Frenchman.

'Well, that's not much!' He was engrossed in his cigar, sucking in its vapours and expelling them over his guests.

'Of course, you must cancel all engagements for this week,' said Bright. 'I presume one of the Sheriffs can stand in for you.'

Threlfall turned an icy eye upon the wiry little policeman. 'In that case you presume too much,' he said. 'Being Lord Mayor is no sinecure. I have perhaps twenty engagements over that period, including five luncheons and four dinners. I am laying down my liver for the Corporation.' He patted his paunch with a little artificial twinkle, to show that he expected a laugh.

Bright obliged, being anxious for co-operation. Losing Sir Peter Hopkirk had not done his own promotion prospects any good either, though he might reasonably, at the age of fifty-one, hope to avoid relegation to Traffic. 'Nevertheless, sir, this man has killed.'

'And?'

'And he may kill again!'

For all his assumed insouciance, it was not easy for Threlfall to hide his unease. 'I *suppose*', he said hesitantly, hiding a tiny quaver in his voice by coughing out some acrid smoke, 'that I *could* insist on all engagements being moved to here. I mean,' here he looked sharply at the two men, 'I'm assuming you can make this building secure?'

Dumeige smiled blandly and fingered his chin, but Bright leant forward, nodding vigorously. 'Of course we could, Lord Mayor. If you will stay in this building for seven days, and not leave, not for *any* purpose, I personally will guarantee your safety.'

'*And after that?*' murmured Dumeige softly, earning himself an angry scowl from Commander Bright.

'After that,' snapped the Commander, 'we shall have this precious Solomon well and truly locked up.'

There was an unexpected noise outside. All three men looked up, startled. It came again, like the handclap of someone slowly applauding.

'What on earth . . . ?' Threlfall pushed a button on his intercom. 'Brigadier!'

'Lord Mayor?' A fuzzy voice, much distorted.

'What's happening outside?'

'It's the man from the opera. He's testing the acoustics.'

'Can't he sing?' Threlfall again posted that gimcrack half-smile, advertising a joke.

'I couldn't say,' crackled the Brigadier.

'I'm going to put a stop to this,' said Bright, standing up abruptly. 'From now on, no one enters this building without full vetting by my team. You agree?' This last he addressed to Dumeige, who seemed intent on polishing his fingernails.

'Oh, I agree,' he said. 'That seems an excellent idea. Really first class.'

Bright flung open the door, almost colliding with a thin young man, perhaps in his early thirties, with lank untidy hair and anxious blue eyes. 'Who are you?'

'I?' The young man gave a half-smile. 'I'm George Sinclair. We're putting on an opera here on Saturday. And . . . er . . . you?'

'Are you indeed?' Bright wasn't quite sure of his ground, but he was absolutely certain that he didn't care for this supercilious character with his ill-fitting grey suit and unpolished shoes. 'Well, I'm Commander Bright of Scotland Yard and you're on your way out, now.'

'Er-hm.'

The Commander turned. The last interjection, more of a clearing of a throat than an actual demurral, had come from alongside him. There he found a very tall man, so tall that the Commander found himself staring at the man's heavy gold-linked watch-chain. 'Yes?'

'I'm Prosper Tabley.' He held out a languid hand.

Now Commanders with responsibility for liaising with Special Branch do not reach such heady positions of authority without some basic facility for recognizing who can be intimidated and who cannot. This man had four things in his favour: his height, the cut of his suit, his Brigade tie and the glacial hint of bags of extra clout in reserve that lay, oh-so-relaxed, behind his polite smile. 'Commander Stephen Bright,' said the little man again, in a subdued tone. ' "P" Division. I hope I can count on your co-operation, sir.'

'Good heavens, yes. Where's Threlfall?'

'Prosper!'

'*There* you are!'

An exhausting round of introductions followed, made all the more trying, for George in particular, since, as Lord Tabley had forgotten his name, he had to cope with being 'Mister-er-you-know', and 'my dear old friend . . . well, there you *are!*' It had one good effect, however, since Commander Bright apparently knew, and was further cowed by, the name of *Lord* Tabley. This put an immediate stopper on his campaign to eject George before he had even reached the Egyptian Hall, the real object of this excursion.

In due course, after an indigestible fifteen minutes of halting reminiscence between Tabley and Threlfall, based on their sharing the same gas-ring at 'school', and momentarily interrupted by Jerry coming through with a form for his master's signature, the little party dawdled south down a marble gallery top-heavy with low-slung crystal chandeliers, past a couple of maroon velvet thrones encrusted with gold, and meandered through double doors into a tall chamber lined with massive white pillars. These, in turn, were holding up a coffered ceiling of obviously colossal weight, but doing so without effort, such was their girth and solidity. If ever a room expressed the twin conceptions of Pomp and Circumstance, this was it.

'May I?' George was beginning to worry about his lunch.

'What?' Threlfall, who had still not entirely understood who George was, posed the question at an angle, not choosing to look straight at him, but rather gazing past him, at some point on the opposite wall.

'Test the acoustics? Clap my hands?'

Threlfall narrowed his eyes. 'If you wish.'

George marched into the centre of the room, and clapped his hands smartly. There was a distant hollow sound, an echo but a muffled one. It was just as he feared. 'Excellent,' he said, turning and smiling confidently at the others. 'No problem at all.'

'Oh good,' said Lord Tabley.

'Is that what you came for?' asked Bright, who hadn't changed his opinion, only his tactics. 'I know you must be very busy.'

George smiled at him too. Officials made him nervous, particularly small foxy ones wearing stained nylon ties, but this was an important contract, and he wasn't going to jeopardize its smooth running for some bad-tempered security guard. 'If you'll just show me where the girls can change,' he said sweetly, 'and where their loo is, I'll get out of your way.'

'I don't think the Commander is that *au fait* with the geography,' said Threlfall, who, seeing the colour mount in Bright's face, was beginning to warm to the young man after all. 'I think your artistes had better change in the Drawing Room if they promise to be careful of the new chairs. I've just had them regilded. That's back the way we came and on the right. Then they can use the oak staircase to reach the new cloakrooms downstairs. How's that?'

'How big's the Drawing Room?' enquired George, pushing his luck.

'Big enough,' said Threlfall, in a dry tone. 'Ah! Here's Brigadier Gooch. He'll show you the way out.'

Chapter Seven

Down to just five days now to cast and rehearse a major opera, George's only chance was either old friends (who would be used to such emergencies) or singers who already knew the parts, *and* in the right language.

Running down the underground escalator, he just caught a westbound Central line train and got off at the first stop, St Paul's. Emerging back into the wintry sunlight, he blinked, and then turned and walked swiftly round the perimeter of the cathedral, oblivious to the Baroque splendour of its towering walls.

'I can't pay you any more,' he muttered. 'That's all there bloody is!' A passing woman turned away quickly, head bent low to avoid eye contact. 'Don't take the fucking job then!' It was a disconcerting quirk of his, to hold arguments in his head in antici- pation of encounters to come, and sometimes to hold them aloud. Running up the broad steps, he bustled past the official collecting admission money, pointing an authoritative finger at some imaginary church dignitary who might be assumed to be waiting for him. 'I've just . . . ' He allowed his voice to trail away, by which time he was well past and into the body of the building.

There was indeed a service in progress, and the hushed prayers of the faithful echoed distantly as if at the far end of a long dark tunnel. The staccato cracks of his footsteps were, by contrast, loud and immediate, drawing indignant looks from hushed tourists as he almost ran down the nave towards the great dome.

'If Isabelle sings *Violetta*, Maria might put up with *Flora* if I promise her a *Fiordiligi* next year. That leaves Jane with the maid, what's-her-name . . . *Annina*!'

'Ssshh!' Some sort of verger, very fat and wearing a red cassock from which emerged an even redder face, had waddled out to meet him, and was standing glowering at him.

'I'm sorry?'

'Divine Service is in progress.'

'I need to speak to Mr Brock.'

The fat man knitted his brows. 'Who?'

'There! That man over there. The tenor with the funny nose.' By good luck, he could actually see the man he sought through a gap in the side-chapel's screen.

'You mean *Screecher*?' The man gaped at him. 'You want me to interrupt Divine Service?'

'If that's what it takes.' George's face took on a determined look as inspiration struck. 'I'm here from Commander Bright of "P" Division. We need Mr Brock over at Headquarters now. I have a patrol car waiting for him outside.'

'But . . . '

'When we spoke to the Dean—'

'The Dean's in there,' said the fat man triumphantly.

'Please let me finish. When we spoke to the Dean's office, they said to find you and—'

'It had better be important,' grumbled the verger, losing heart. Crossing to a pillar, he collected a tall brass rod of office and, holding it before his stomach, he walked majestically through into the midst of the worshippers and up to where Rupert Brock, a tenor who had often worked for George, was preparing to sing a canticle, and whispered in his ear. Rupert's face swivelled ninety degrees, and George signalled him with a significant nod. Rupert shook his head energetically, and others started to look round, but the verger must have said something more persuasive, because Rupert put down his Psalter and, with a look of resigned martyrdom, followed the verger out of the congregation, pausing only to genuflect towards the altar as he emerged under the arch.

'What the hell . . . '

'SShh!' whispered George. 'Divine Service.'

'What's so bloody important?'

'I need you to sing *Gastone* and cover *Alfredo* this Saturday, rehearsing from nine-thirty day after tomorrow.'

Rupert took a step back. 'Are you telling me you've put my job here on the line to ask me to sing bloody *Gastone*?'

'One hundred pounds in cash.'

'Done.' The young man turned on his heel and walked back into the congregation, adding his voice in a high caterwaul, 'Oh ye cataracts and ye *fountains . . .*'

'You were having me on, weren't you?' hissed the verger, suddenly at George's shoulder again. '*Patrol car! Headquarters!* This is the City of London not downtown San Francisco.'

George smiled at him. 'I could see you were a man who liked a laugh.'

The fat man smiled back. 'Ten pounds or a trip to the security office. That's my idea of a real laugh.'

George handed over a banknote. 'For the roof,' he said, and hurried back down the aisle.

The official at the door stopped him. 'Were you planning to pay the admission, sir? I'm afraid we have to insist.'

George nodded. 'I absolutely understand. In fact that verger over there asked me for ten pounds. Is that enough?'

The man's face darkened. '*That* man?'

'Yes. He put it up his left sleeve,' added George helpfully. 'A ten-pound note.'

'Wait here, please, sir.' The official started towards the fat verger, giving George the chance to slip unobtrusively out through the cathedral door.

Back down to the underground trains, and his next call was a bar off Leicester Square, where he sat down at a rickety table enriched with a red and white gingham cloth complete with ketchup stains and ordered a Bailey's with ice. He didn't have to wait long.

'What are *you* doing here?' A svelte woman in black lycra trousering and a white diamanté top came sliding round from behind the bar.

George stood up awkwardly as she hugged him effusively. 'Jane, darling.'

'*Hello!*' she said. 'You want something!'

'How are you and Ed fixed for this week?'

'Ed?' She wrinkled her brows.

'Yes, Ed. Your husband. Edmund Pusey Nuneham of Number 3, Station Approach, Reigate.'

'Oh, *him.*' She smiled, rather coldly.

'Exactly. I've got a sudden gig on Saturday. Money no object. *Traviata* with all the trimmings.'

'Money no *object* . . . ?'

'A hundred and fifty each and three hundred for the costumes.'

She whistled. 'For *Traviata*? For all those people? This Saturday!'

'It's not the bloody *Ring*, Jane.'

'Four hundred and fifty.'

'For *nine* people. All you've got to do is hire six sets of tails, three nice frocks and a maid's costume.'

'Then I've got to make them fit, I suppose?'

'And sing *Annina*,' said George, bracing himself.

'I'm sorry?'

'And sing *Annina*.' He smiled winningly.

'The fucking *maid*! God, I hate that smile,' she said nastily. 'Someone must have told you it's winning. Actually, it's foul. Four hundred for the costumes and I'll sing the maid. Who's Ed singing? The butler, I suppose?'

'*Doctor Grenvil.*'

'So that's seven hundred all in. Deal?'

'Deal!' He leant across and kissed her cheek.

'Who's this?' A giant shadow fell across the table.

'Hello, treasure. This is George Sinclair. He runs an opera company.'

'Hello,' said George nervously. The man had the size, shape and smell of a gorilla. He looked George over and evidently decided he was no competition. Without replying, he just turned on his heel and retreated through the fly curtain at the back of the bar. 'Phew!'

'He's a lamb,' cooed Jane in a soft voice.

'I don't doubt it,' said George. 'See you at St Seraphina's on Wednesday.'

'Wednesday! That's only three days' rehearsal. Why can't we start tomorrow with whoever you've got?'

'Because,' he said, 'the hall wasn't free until Wednesday. Anyway, it gives you a whole free day for all those costumes.' She shook her head and grinned. 'See you then. Nine thirty on the dot. You'll tell Ed?' She nodded.

He was half way out the door when she called out, 'Where?'

'Where?'

'Where's the show?'

'The Mansion House, London EC4!' Five down, and four to go.

Chapter Eight

Solomon himself was not quite as confident as the image he sought to present. Just as Threlfall, his latest target, was subject to considerable if intermittent attacks of icy panic, so the hunter, sitting now at a desk in a small hotel room east of Tower Bridge, was cursing himself for setting so precise a timescale *again*. It was his besetting vice, these bursts of overconfidence. Or did he need this pressure to bring out his genius for sensational improvisation.

On the desk, a small tape recorder was playing an aria from *Martha*, but not too loud. Next to it, a small laptop computer was connected to a mobile telephone, and from its screen he had spent the last twenty minutes taking some very precise notes. Really, people in his position, people with other people to *kill*, had much to be grateful for. The technological advances of the last few years had delivered to him, and no doubt to many others, the innermost secrets of places like the Home Office and New Scotland Yard. In fact it had been Brigadier

Gooch's computer that he had just been inspecting. Such menus! Such guest-lists! All the City's fattest calves killed, and all for the City's fattest men!

A glimpse in the mirror caught him smiling. God what a wonderful smile! He felt quite sick with desire to share that smile with someone supple, and soft, and yielding.

Later. Later he would telephone that special number, and have someone *very* yielding sent along to submit. In this mood, she could expect some pretty startling demands. Meanwhile he had things to consider.

Stabbing Hopkirk in the throat had been rather rash. He might have got blood all over his shirt-front, for example. Leaning back in his chair, he clasped his arms behind his neck and indulged in a little nostalgia. Hanging Tait had been quite extra-ordinarily satisfactory. He had got into the Park Avenue building by dressing up as the banker's neighbour, an old lady with bow legs and spinal trouble. Tait had actually asked him in for a cocktail. Three hours he'd played with him. *Three hours.* He'd never been so exhausted. Whereas von Arnim he'd shot as the old man ran at him, shot him squarely in the belly and then in his screaming scarlet mouth.

Whatever people might say about those old Prussian castles, they certainly knew how to build solid walls. When he'd let himself out, still dressed as von

Arnim's chauffeur, no one seemed to have heard a thing. And now all he had to do was the same again with Threlfall, and it would be over. All four, justly recompensed.

Over! He laughed out loud at such an absurd idea. For he was loving it. *Loving* it. The thrills, the chase, the stalking and then, dear God, the killing. Justice had had to be done, but he had had no idea that it would also be *fun*. There was no way he was going to stop now. It would just be a case of finding new targets. But first things first. After Threlfall, the world!

He had already had a chance to observe the new precautions taken outside the Mansion House. There was an armed and uniformed policeman at each of the two main doors and a third in the alley at the back, near the emergency exits. Another two patrolled the perimeter, checking on their colleagues, and a City of London Police van was parked ostentatiously across the way in Walbrook. All the better, he thought. They'll be too confident. Whereas I . . . the strain was too much. He lifted the receiver and dialled the mobile number.

'How may I help you, sir?' enquired a husky female voice.

'This is John Smith,' he said. 'I have an account with you.'

'Of course, Mr Smith. Thank you for calling us. Just tell me what you would like tonight.'

He listed his requirements and then went into the hotel bathroom to prepare for his evening's entertainment.

At the same time, only a few hundred yards north, Commander Bright was reviewing security inside the Mansion House with the Lord Mayor's portly Private Secretary, Brigadier Gooch, he whose computer programmes had just been systematically raped.

Bright had established that the resident staff of six consisted of the Steward, Mr Edwards, a tall asthmatic man in his seventies, who lived alone in a small flat in the attic. He had the supervision of the footmen, Frederick, Peter and Dennis, housed in three small rooms above Mrs Threlfall's bedroom. Since the catering was all contracted out to the Standish Banqueting Company, that left only the two housemaids, Gwladys and Dorothy, who shared a second small flat next to Mr Edwards.

'They'd better move out until this is over,' said Bright, making a note on his pad.

Gooch glared at him. 'That's impossible,' he barked. 'My secretaries have spent the day shifting all the Lord Mayor's engagements to here. We have a luncheon and a dinner every night, seven investitures, five charity board meetings and the Lord Mayor of Vienna for a ceremonial tea. I can vouch for all six myself. Edwards has been here since he was fifteen.'

Bright shook his head. 'I'm sorry . . . '

'I'm sorry too,' interrupted Gooch, standing up. 'There's no question of these people being further disrupted. We have tried to co-operate over the stationing of your men inside the building. The catering manager entirely understands about his people being vetted and issued with daily security passes. But if you want to make an issue of this, I and my staff will withdraw from the whole process. I shall go and explain this to the Lord Mayor before clearing my desk.'

'*Brigadier!*' Bright raised his hands in mock surrender, realizing he had achieved all he could. Indeed he had done better than he had expected, with a command post on each floor, video cameras to be installed in every corridor and in the main State Rooms, and an undertaking that everyone, including the Brigadier himself, would be comprehensively searched on entering, and on leaving, the building. 'You've been marvellous, and of course I bow to your superior experience.' Bright tried a smile, and Gooch tried one back. 'Now it's up to us to put it all into practice. Thanks to you, the Lord Mayor will live to see Christmas!'

*

The great man himself was, did they but know it, poised precisely fifteen feet above where they sat, seated in front of his computer, tapping fruitlessly as he watched the scrolling screen with angry blood-shot eyes.

'*Nothing!* There's nothing here at all.'

Jerry, his angular assistant, looked up from another screen where he was busily rewriting their most recent financial transactions with a view to presenting a bowdlerized version should any snooping Fraud Squaddies hit upon this particular trail.

Threlfall snarled something inaudible, then snapped, 'Try it again.'

Jerry tapped some keys and the image came up on both their screens: a total blank.

Then, before their horrified eyes, a message was slowly typed out across the screen:

W.e.l.c.o.m.e .t.o .t.h.e . . . W.a.l.k.i.n.g . . . D.e.a.d . . 5 . . . d.a.y.s . . . m.a.x.i.m.u.m . . .

'What. . . . ?' Threlfall's face had lost all its ver-milion ruddiness. Indeed he had turned a most alarming shade of greasy grey. 'I . . . , I . . . '

But Jerry was paying no attention. Jerry was busy himself, a triumphant grin on his lopsided fea-tures. 'The fool!' he hissed, as he stabbed at his keyboard and juggled the telephone handset. 'The complacent self-satisfied idiot! This exchange will drive me mad. No, here we are! The Black Friar

Hotel.' And before the Lord Mayor could answer or comment on his strange assistant's exultation, the little man had thrown back the bolts on the further door, and vanished down the service staircase that led to the kitchen.

Chapter Nine

What had happened was that Solomon's visitor, a slender black girl with 'Hello!' tattooed on her left buttock, had proved such an outstanding success in satisfying, even indeed anticipating, his wishes, that he had eventually shown her to the door in a state of almost transcendental euphoria. Hurrying back to get dressed for his next commitment, he had, while pulling on his overcoat, noticed the computer still attached to his mobile phone. While unplugging it, he had suddenly given way to a hilarious urge to give Threlfall another little surprise. Plugging the machine into the hotel telephone socket, he had swiftly hacked his way via the now familiar route into Jerry's apparatus. It may have achieved maximum effect against Threlfall, in that the Lord Mayor had actually watched his message emerging on to his screen, but it had a drawback too.

When he emerged from the lift and raised a cheery hand to the hotel receptionist, he did not notice the bent silhouette of Jerry, who had hurried into the hotel and hidden in one of the telephone booths in the lobby. The latter gave a silent whistle, and, drawing back deeper into the shadows, waited for half a minute before edging out of his lair and scurrying out into the darkening street in time to see his quarry pausing by the steps of Tower Hill station before turning to walk down Bristol Street.

At the same time as Jerry settled down to follow Solomon at a discreet distance, Isabelle Morny, once George's lover, was in her bath, humming a snatch of some foreign folk song as she soaped her body. She was, by a strange mischance, also his half-sister. Their mothers, both sopranos, had both been bedded by the famous conductor Victor Szelko as a prelude to their marrying the respective 'fathers', a variation on the theme of 'taking an interest in young singers' which the wily old Austrian had perfected over a long, and arduous, career.

While there was no actual evidence to prove their kinship, they themselves had little doubt of it, and this cast a grey dubious shadow over what had already become a difficult relationship after only a few months. Isabelle herself was troubled by few scruples, least of all those which interfered with her enjoyment of life. George, however, being naturally inhibited, was much troubled by the unlucky coincidence. It was not that he loved, or desired, her any the less, just that he felt unable to overcome his scruples. She heard the outer door. 'Any luck?'

'Hmm?' He was already heading for the drinks' cupboard.

'What was the room like, *chéri?*'

'Fine.'

'So we're doing it?'

'We certainly are! I've cashed the cheque.'

She giggled and disappeared under the water. When she reappeared, he was sitting on the side of the bath, draining a large glass of vodka and tonic. 'I shall sing *Violetta?*'

'Of course.' He smiled down at her. She really was a very beautiful young woman. It was just that . . .

'Did you get Jane?'

'I certainly did. And Rupert.'

'Oh God! Not for *Alfredo?* I'm not singing if . . . '

'Don't panic!' He laid a hand on her slippery shoulder, and immediately felt a stab of physical desire. 'He's agreed to do *Gastone.*'

'Was Ed with Jane?'

'No.' He laughed. 'She had some sort of body-builder in tow.'

'She likes them big,' said Isabelle, reaching up and touching him.

'Isabelle . . . ' He was almost crying with frustration.

'Sorry.' She smiled apologetically. 'Alasdair's taking me to *L ' Elisir d'Amore.*'

'God!' He started to lose his temper and then said, 'With Pavarotti?' She nodded. 'Oh, darling, you *are* lucky,' he said, losing his self-pity in the importance of such an occasion for Isabelle. 'You've always wanted to hear him sing *Nemorino!*'

'I know!' She smiled up at him.

He bent and kissed the top of her head with real fervour. 'Is Winston coming round tomorrow?' It was another oddity in their relationship that she was actually only recently married to another singer, a black baritone without a work permit whom she had rescued from deportation by this drastic solution. Since such arrangements are viewed with some suspicion by the Home Office, her husband had to pay her regular visits to sustain the fiction that they were cohabiting in wedded bliss.

'Pass me the towel,' she said, standing up in the bath. 'I've spoken to him. He'll sing *Germont* for you. And Bruno rang by chance, so I've roped him in as *Baron Douphol*. You can't say I don't love you!'

'I'm very lucky,' he said with a wry grin. 'So what did you say I'd pay?'

'A hundred to Bruno, two hundred to Winston. Starting Wednesday morning.'

'*Two hundred to Winston?*'

'Well . . . ' She pouted at him and placed one slender finger on his cheek. 'He *is* my husband.'

There was nothing to say to this. 'So who've you got lined up for *Alfredo* and the *Marchese?*'

She shrugged her naked shoulders. 'Who knows?' Outside, a deep-toned car horn sounded. *'Mon Dieu!* There's Alasdair. I must run. He doesn't like being kept waiting!'

George swallowed a sneer. 'Mister Big, eh? Isn't he a bit young to be knighted? What does he *do* anyway?'

Isabelle shrugged. 'He's a lawyer. And he's not a knight. He inherited it. He's a baron something.'

'Oh!' said George in exaggerated deference. 'A *baronet*. Silly me.'

'I don't like it when you're like this,' said Isabelle, staring at him sadly. 'I love you. Not Alasdair. Sir or no sir.' She turned away.

George went back into the bedroom and, throwing himself upon his blood-red satin sheets, he reached for the video tuner. Another night with *Rosenkavalier*. It could be worse, he thought. At least Isabelle would be coming back to him.

Yet he was still watching the video, for the second time, when he finally dozed off around four in the morning. Isabelle had not come home.

Chapter Ten

Noon the next day found the Lady Mayoress, Mrs Reginald Threlfall, still in bed. As a matter of fact, Mrs Reginald Threlfall usually spent her mornings in bed, and sometimes, depending on the exact nature of her breakfast, the afternoons as well.

As Charlotte Fitzgerald she was still remembered as a great beauty, a debutante whose delicate profile and creamy complexion had driven two generations of young men to paroxysms of throbbing desire. Yet she had married Reggie Threlfall, by no means the best looking or richest of her suitors, and when asked (with some hesitation) by her friends *exactly* what had been the clinching factor in his favour, she generally had replied, '*Dear* Reggie. He was always kind to my horse.'

For hunting, first with the Bicester and latterly (when Daddy had made good, or, rather, better) with the Quorn, had been the central (some said the only) focus of her young life. There had been no shortage of money, she had even scored a B in her French

A level; in fact she had seemed set for a lifetime's happiness divided between Sloane Street and Melton Mowbray. So why, at the age of only forty-nine, was she drinking her breakfast out of a gin bottle?

Marriage! That great institution which half the world travels hopefully towards, while the other half dreams hopefully of escape. People might say, indeed they did, that George's relationship with Isabelle lacked conventional bottom. But Charlotte's relationship with her husband had been a bottomless well of disaster from Day One. She hadn't known much about him, except that his uncle was an Earl and there was *money*. But while other, younger, suitors whispered about *sex*, and, ironically, boasted of how much they drank at parties, Reggie Threlfall just quietly fed her hunter sugar-lumps and looked soulfully out of his large brown eyes into her sharp bright sapphire ones.

So they'd got married. Friday the First of May: St Peter's, Eaton Square! Claridge's! Heathrow, a flight to Venice and a powerboat to the Danieli on the moonlit wedding-night! *Bliss.* But then: clothes torn off, drunken scenes of violent penetration, drunken scenes, indeed, of bestial deviancy: less, oh so much less than bliss; more like bloody murder, in fact. So for thirty years her husband had spent his time and money on prostitutes, and she had had to make do . . . with gin!

Her complexion had gone, leaving a ripe moonscape with heavy pores and scarlet veins. Her figure was going despite a food-free diet, here a sag, there a bulge, rippling mutinously under the Hardy Amies suitings. Only her eyes, those magnificent blue sapphires that had pierced the hearts of so many, still shone bravely from the battlefield, lonely beacons of her long-lost dreams.

A discreet knock and Peter, the footman whose job each year was to tend the current Lady Mayoress, slipped quietly into the room to gather yesterday's discarded clothing. 'Tuesday the Twentieth, and another one of those horrible fogs!' he ventured, summing up her sobriety-quota with one quick analytical glance: poor soul.

'Bloody things!' She gave a loud laugh.

Peter sighed inwardly. He'd had some tricky ones in his time, but Mrs Threlfall was the worst so far, just as Reggie Threlfall had won the domestic staff's prize for the Ultimate All-Time Worst Lord Mayor in Living Memory.

It was not just having to put up with the man's gross eating habits, as he drooled and spat his way through mounds of food at every meal. It was not even the outrageous indignity of having part of 'their' building, their beloved Mansion House, in this case the Lord Mayor's dressing room, turned into a no-go area by the fitting of new locks. But having to clear everything with the weird Jerry, who took it upon himself to outrank even Brigadier Gooch in organizing the Lord Mayor's day was, as his colleague Frederick was wont to say, 'really gross'.

And now they had the police swarming all over the building, setting up cameras, even screwing things into the walls, not that you could blame this 'Solomon' man for wanting to do away with the Lord Mayor, him and half the occupants of the Mansion House was how Peter saw it.

'You have the Gold and Silver Wire-Drawers Ladies Committee coming for lunch, m'lady,' he murmured, though loud enough to make sure that she heard, while deftly collecting last night's dress for Gwladys to iron.

'You can't be serious.'

'Twelve thirty in the Morning Room. There's only eight of them,' he said, trying to encourage her. A kind man at heart, and nearly thirty though he looked no more than sixteen, he could readily appreciate that thirty years with this particular Lord Mayor must have taken its toll. 'Mrs Bellew is the President. She's a nice lady, very colourful.'

'Does she wear gold and silver wire drawers?' she enquired with another of her disconcerting guffaws.

'I really couldn't say, m'lady.' He withdrew, rather hurt. But there was no doing with some people, and he had more than enough to do helping Dennis and Frederick lay up two lunches, one in the Private Dining Room and the other in the Parlour for the Court of Aldermen now that they were coming to the Mansion House instead of to Guildhall as planned.

The same hour found George, his face red and crumpled from sleeping late, angrily brushing his teeth. Swilling the acrid scum round his mouth, he stared mournfully into the mirror. Where are the horns, he wondered. I'm looking at the face of a deliberate cuckold. My woman, whom I can't touch, has been tarting about with a merchant banker who looks like a fucking totem-pole and probably—

'That's my toothbrush!'

He'd never even heard her come in. 'So?' He tried to put a wealth of meaning into the word, but succeeded only in having to wipe a foamy dribble from the side of his mouth.

'So? *So?*' She gave a deliciously light laugh and, rising on her tiptoes, kissed him warmly. 'While you have been snoring, I, your little sister, have been working on your behalf!'

'In or out of costume?'

'*Ah, non! C'est pas gentil, ça!*' Yet she was still laughing behind the mock outrage. 'I knew you would think the worst of your Isabelle, baring all for a square meal!'

He took her hand and led her back to the bed. 'Sit down.'

She sat meekly beside him, looking up at the crumpled face. 'Yes?'

'I love you. Last night was torture for me, imagining you in that filthy man's sweaty arms.' He wiped his forehead.

'See! It is you who are sweaty! Did you know it was Alasdair who got us the Mansion job?'

'Mansion House job,' he corrected, staring. 'How?'

She shrugged. 'He knew you hadn't got much work. He knows some lord or something. He likes you.'

'He likes you more.'

She nodded. 'He's not a homo, that is certain.' She chuckled.

'What?'

'What?'

'What's funny?'

She met his gaze with an absolutely candid blue stare. 'You are. And Alasdair. He wanted me so much. And, truly, would it have been so dreadful?' She reached out and held him firmly with both hands as he tried to rise. 'No! No, I didn't. Because I love you, and because I knew it would hurt you.'

He stared down at her, trying to judge the fearless light in her eyes. 'You didn't?'

She shook her head. 'No.'

'No sex?'

'No.'

'No kissing?'

'No.'

'No fondling?'

'*Quoi?*'

'You didn't let him touch you . . . anywhere . . . ?'

She stared at him. 'I held his hand.'

'Nothing else?'

'*Mon Dieu!* You are impossible. I tell you everything.'

'So where did you spend the night?'

'On his sofa. I had far too much of his excellent *crème de menthe.*'

'Did he run you home?' She looked puzzled. 'Did he drive you here this morning?'

She shook her head. 'His driver, Stefan, brought me here. Alasdair works harder than we do. He has to be in front of his computer by seven o'clock!'

'Greedy bastard!' But he was mollified and standing up, he walked, straighter now, back to the mirror to shave, thus missing the look of amused irony in her guileless blue eyes. Men! They'll believe anything, even the most blatant untruths, rather than risk damaging their delicate *amour propre.* 'I've had no luck with tenors!' he shouted over the sound of the gushing tap.

'Have you tried the agencies?'

'Are you *mad?*' He appeared in the doorway, face half covered in foam. 'I'd have to pay union rates!'

She shrugged her shoulders. 'With only a *week* . . . '

'I know.' He slumped against the door-jamb. 'But I've rung everyone I can think of.'

'Ted?'

'He's doing something at the Albert Hall.'

'Frangio?'

'Him! Remember what his top notes were like?'

'At least he had top notes!' She giggled. 'You're right. What about Gaspard?'

'No reply. In fact I think his phone's been cut off. It's the usual story. When there's no clients, they're all round asking for a job. When I get a client—'

'When *I* get one you mean!' she put in, grinning.

'Yes, yes!' He hugged her to him, oblivious of the effect of the shaving foam on her hair. 'You're wonderful.'

She disengaged herself and crossed to the dressing table. 'Who else are we missing?'

'Just the *Marchese*. Surely I can find a deadbeat baritone anywhere, but nobody's bloody answering.'

'Do you actually need him?'

George thought. 'Well, he has a couple of lines, one saying hello to *Alfredo*, and another gossiping about him, so I suppose not. I was going to get him to understudy Winston as *Germont* but maybe we could take a risk. Or maybe Bruno . . . ?'

She shook her head. 'Don't even try. He thinks

he should be singing *Germont*. You're very lucky he's agreed to do *Baron Douphol*.'

'I know. Perhaps they're the wrong way round.'

'Poor Winston. I owe him something.'

'Why? You got him his work permit by marrying him, *and* you took him to bed.'

'Only once.'

'So you say.' His temper was beginning to rise again, and he turned away, sick with jealousy. She seemed so slight, so defenceless, and yet she had as formidable a power to cause him pain as she had once given him pleasure. 'I'd better get shaved. I *will* try those damned agents.'

Chapter Eleven

After Solomon had left the hotel the night before, Jerry had followed him on foot through the dark streets for nearly half an hour. Apart from one nasty moment, when he had come round a corner to find his quarry staring into a brightly lit Fleet Street shopfront only a few feet away, he had kept a very respectful distance and was quite satisfied that the man who had threatened to kill his employer was wholly unaware that his identity had been discovered.

Should he call the police? He slipped into a small pub and sat in a corner booth, nursing a small whisky. The idea had no attractions whatever. All his life, Jerry had been taught to regard information as a commodity, to be sold or bartered as aggressively as, say, copper futures or gold bullion. And this was hot news indeed.

The question was: to whom was it worth most? In real terms the answer was Threlfall, since it was his life that the man wanted. But the Lord Mayor would hardly expect a man who had worked for him for nearly twenty years, twenty very profitable years, to demand payment for identifying his would-be killer.

In some ways, the most profitable solution lay in keeping quiet, or even in assisting the man in his plan. Threlfall dead left only one man aware of the true extent and whereabouts of his criminal earnings. These were very great. Jerry with his six-figure nest egg could look forward to a continuing life of ease. Jerry with sole access to his master's eight-figure deposit account *as well* was looking at retirement in luxury indeed.

He shivered and sipped at the drink. What about Solomon himself. What was his anonymity worth to him? Nothing in the newspaper reports suggested that he would be an easy man to blackmail. On the contrary, anything like that would have to be handled with extreme care. Looking around cautiously, he paid for his drink and sidled back into the darkened street.

Half an hour's brisk walking back the way he'd come brought him to the Walbrook door of the Mansion House.

'What do you want?' One of the uniformed constables had stepped towards him, while the other had dropped his hand surreptitiously on to the butt of his revolver.

'Jerry Tomkins. Lord Mayor's Personal Assistant.'

'Where's your pass?'

'What pass?'

'The Commander issued everyone in there with passes this afternoon.' He could hear people getting out of the plain car parked across the street.

'Not to me, he didn't,' whined Jerry angrily. 'I came out through the kitchen door just after six.'

'Who does he say he is?' This new policeman was carrying an automatic pistol, the sort of weapon Jerry fantasized about after watching the latest Sylvester Stallone adventure on screen.

'Tomkins. Works for LM.'

The man scanned a list. 'There's a Tomkins here. First name?'

'Jerry. Gerald.' He found himself scanning the busy streets. What if Solomon had spotted him? These clowns were making him an easy target. 'You must know who I am!'

'Must we?' The first policeman was losing patience. 'Man with no pass. You'd better go over to that van.' He pointed to an ominous black furniture van drawn up facing down towards Cannon Street. They'll take your details and check them there.'

'But it's urgent . . . '

'It always is,' said the policeman wearily. He'd had a drunken Mrs Threlfall earlier in the evening, demanding entrance into 'my house, you frightful little man!' She hadn't had a pass either. 'Move along, please.'

71

If Solomon had been watching this scene, he would certainly have been smiling. All in all, it took an increasingly distraught Jerry two hours to get back into the building, by which time the Threlfalls were well into a ceremonial dinner with his fellow Aldermen and their wives, and, in one case, husband.

Taking advantage of this diversion, Jerry spent a more profitable two hours rewriting some of the programmes on the Lord Mayor's personal computer and putting through a number of related communications to contacts both inside and outside the country. At ten thirty, hearing sounds of coffee being taken through to the Private Dining Room next door, he tidied up the desk, carefully erased the relevant BAK files and settled down at his own terminal to continue to confuse the trail of some of their more questionable transactions in the past.

'Where the hell did you go?' The Lord Mayor was back, and in no good mood either, though his face was mottled with fine wine.

Jerry shrugged. 'False alarm. I thought I could trace the bugger.'

'No luck?' Threlfall peered at him suspiciously. He didn't like his little assistant, with his whining ways and crooked walk. Nor did he altogether trust him, despite the very high rewards flowing from their shared career of financial chicanery.

'Not a sausage.'

Threlfall loomed over Jerry's shoulder, a menacing bulk which set the little man shivering again. 'You wouldn't be thinking of profiting from this bastard's threats, would you?' he enquired heavily. 'Because just in case you do, I've made my own arrangements. Lose me, and you lose everything, including your freedom.'

So! 'You can rely on me,' said Jerry, without looking up. At least that had made his mind up for him. He was getting out, with the maximum booty and the minimum delay.

Having established the probable source of the threats against Threlfall, he could see no useful purpose in exposing the man. True, he had briefly contemplated raising a little extra capital by placing a price on his silence. But that had been only a very short-lived moment of madness. A man who had killed thrice already was hardly likely to submit peacefully to blackmail! But he needed three clear working days for his transactions to be complete. Whatever else happened, by this time Thursday evening he was going to be on his way south, to Buenos Aires, where, unknown to his employer, he already had a sizeable investment in two new shopping malls.

Chapter Twelve

Tuesday was a busy day for many people. Commander Bright and his team spent all day perfecting the surveillance systems within the Mansion House and programming a new computer section in the basement, complete with fresh psychological data on everyone involved, however loosely, with Solomon and his three previous victims. George just sat by his telephone, ringing round colleagues, acquaintances and, finally, agents and even competitors, in a fruitless search for a good Italianate tenor. The Threlfalls, husband and wife, paced their palatial temporary home, doing their best to avoid each other, while Mr Edwards, the Steward, sought to encourage his already overworked staff with the thought of the overtime rates they were clocking up in ministering to the Lord Mayor in his hour of need. Jerry, confined by his own choice to his bedsitter next to Mr Edwards' apartment, remained in his room, avoiding them all.

Paul Dumeige had his own agenda, and little was

seen of him either by Scotland Yard, or by their colleagues in the City of London Police, while the Tableys, secure in the knowledge that a performance would take place, with the tickets all sold, and the charity sure to be suitably grateful, felt able to relax with a day's shopping.

Wednesday morning, as the strange triangular clock struck nine on the narrow concrete spire of St Seraphina's, West Fulham, George parked his battered orange Citroën deux-chevaux in the space normally reserved for the Incumbent, a friar of doughty girth with a reputation for divinely inspired utterances.

George, however, was aware that the great man was away on his annual pilgrimage to a luxurious hotel on Lake Ullswater, so he reversed up against the hedge with perfect confidence.

'Good morning!' The Nunehams, Ed and Jane, came walking round the corner of the church, hand in hand.

'Good morning!' George had been in the music business for too long to be surprised by how anybody behaved, least of all married couples.

There was something about 'opera' as a concept, and as a career, that seemed to bring an element of exaggeration to everything that touched it, even in the modest way in which his ad-hoc company, and those involved in it, worked.

'Hi there!' Ed Nuneham, big, beefy and sweating under a twenty-ounce herringbone tweed, raised one ham of a hand. 'Back in business, I see.'

George nodded. One of the reasons he could undercut his many competitors was the Nunehams, who could both sing and work backstage in an unusual combination. While Ed stage-managed, carting about the heavy props and lighting, Jane could sew and fit the costumes, advise on make-up and fix the other singers' hair, all while learning and later performing her own role or roles. He could undercut his competitors, but as a matter of fact, he didn't. He just kept a bigger slice of the profit instead. Indeed, as he frequently explained out loud to an empty room when imagining an angry con-frontation with one of his singers, he *had* to, with his sister to support now as well as make his own way in a murky world.

'We're still short of *Alfredo* and the *Marchese*,' said George, with something of a question in his voice.

The other two looked at each other. 'Bruno?' tried Ed, wrinkling his forehead with the effort.

'He's singing *Baron Douphol*,' said his wife snap-pishly. 'I *told* you that in the car! You never listen.'

Ed rubbed his head. 'Actually I've been having trouble with my ears,' he said to George. 'Doctor Wotsit thinks it's from when I was in the army. Hello! there's Rupert.'

The little tenor from St Paul's waved merrily as he

sped past them on his moped and swung it round the side of George's car and brought it to a quiet halt next to some railings. 'Morning all!' He took out a heavy chain and wound it through the rear wheel before padlocking it to the stanchion. He came over and patted George's sleeve. 'You really pissed Alan off!'

'Who's Alan?'

'Mister Impossible. The verger who got me out of the service for you. He's been suspended, thanks to you. He really wants your home address in a big way. I had to say you were based in Cardiff, but you'd better watch your back. He's got a really nasty temper, and he's done time.'

'That's no surprise. He wanted a bribe. In a *cathedral*. I wasn't letting him get away with that!'

Jane laughed out loud. 'George the Incorruptible. That's a new one. Have you tried Billy Frangio?'

'Don't be absurd. He's *inaudible* in a normal room. We're talking about a room the size of a bloody ship!'

'Acoustics?'

'None.'

'I bet you didn't tell them that!'

'Of course not. We all needed the job.'

'For that,' said Jane dryly, 'read George and Isabelle need the job.'

'Anybody here point me in the direction of George Sinclair?'

They all four turned at the sound of a fruity

authoritative voice. It originated from an unexpected source, a bent character, almost a tramp, who was making his way awkwardly towards them.

George took a step towards him. 'That's me,' he said, with just a tremor of apprehension. It was the eyes of the man. They had something unsettling about them, something *knowing*.

'Someone said you wanted a baritone.'

'I do. Who said?'

'My agent. Lily at Benson and Benson's. She said you'd be here.'

'Can you sing?'

'I will if someone can play. I've brought *Sei voi ballare* and *Di Provenza*.' The scores were sticking out of his seedy old jacket's pocket.

'It's the *Marchese* I'm looking for,' said George repressively, and the man's face fell.

'She said you wanted *Germont père*,' he complained. 'I'd never have come . . . '

George took him by the arm and walked out of earshot. 'A hundred in cash,' he said, 'and another fifty if you cover the father.'

'Any learning fee?' asked the man slyly.

'Christ! You drive a hard bargain. A tenner but don't tell the others.'

'One sixty in cash up front?'

George laughed. 'Certainly not. Fifty up front at the dress rehearsal and the rest after I've been paid. This is touring opera, not the bloody Met.'

The man straightened a little, gaining confidence perhaps, and shook George's hand. 'I'm Henry Timpson,' he said. 'Late of Kent Opera and, after they folded, the Opéra de Nantes.'

'What did you sing for Kent?' asked George, interested.

'Just chorus, old boy. That's my natural hole. But I do come up for air occasionally, just to show the punters there's life in Henry Timpson yet!' He coughed, a raucous hacking explosion of repetitive sound, and then wiped his mouth on a scarlet handkerchief.

'You've got a right one there,' murmured Ed when he and George had a moment together. 'You should have at least heard him sing.'

George shook his head. 'Who cares if the *Marchese* can sing. All he's got to do is stand there and look lecherous.'

'Isn't he covering Winston?'

'Yes, but that doesn't matter. Winston'd never miss a show.'

'But what would you do if he did?'

'Ed! The guy can sing. He was with Kent Opera for God's sake.'

Ed shook his head. 'You're the boss,' he said.

The next people to arrive were Isabelle, who, in the interests of public wifeliness, had taken a bus to join her husband at his flat in Battersea, and Winston himself, spread largely behind the wheel of an ancient Chevrolet Impala, all chrome and banked braking lights.

'The *happy couple*,' murmured Rupert sourly. No one had married him just as a favour, nor had they ever done anything else for him that he could remember. His whole life, by his own account, had been spent doing favours for other people for nil return. No wonder he needed the occasional *sip* of something refreshing, just to stop him from sitting down and *howling*. Bravely, he wiped his eye and turned discreetly into the men's toilet. There he pulled a little cylindrical flask from his sock and unscrewed the gun-metal cap.

'Not before six!' said a voice.

He started violently. '*Look!*' he shouted. 'You've made me spill it!'

Ed chuckled. He'd gone ahead to hide in the lavatory for precisely this purpose. 'Teach you not to drink in company time. You can swim in bloody gin in your own time, but while you're being paid in this outfit, no noggins, clear?'

'It's vodka, actually,' sniffed Rupert. 'Gin is for old farts like—'

Ed loomed over him. 'I drink gin,' he said. 'Sparingly. In a glass. With ice and Vermouth. Not sucked out of a metal willie and dribbling down my chin. Now get out there and sing something before I do something I might regret. You've got the next line in the opera in case you've forgotten.'

'*In Alfredo Germont, o signora, ecco un altro che molto v'onora . . .* ' warbled the tenor, his voice palpitating uncertainly as his Adam's apple squeezed painfully up and down his elongated throat.

'Well, whatever,' groaned Ed dismissively.

'I can't sing it if there's no *Alfredo*,' said Rupert, 'now can I?'

'Doesn't sound to me as if you could sing it with half a gross of *Alfredos* stretching as far as the eye can see,' said Ed. 'So you can be grateful that I didn't do the casting!'

'George is very conscious of how much I've done for him.'

'Look!' Ed was tired. 'Just get out there and do what you're paid for.' And he hustled the little tenor through the swing door and into the rehearsal hall, a highly decorated eighteenth-century cube of a room, in marked contrast to the mean little modernist concrete tub of a church to which it was still attached.

'Once again!' called Jane. 'Now we've got Rupert!'

There they were, all five of them, the chorus of the Floria Tosca Grand Opera Company, one of the many peripatetic groups who earned a precarious living by selling their services as entertainers in that most demanding of professions, opera singers: little Rupert, reedily nasal, with his face already marked by the blotched veins of a drinking man, the massive Ed, stalwart in tweeds, his eyes forever brooding on Jane, the wife he could never understand or keep from straying, Henry the newcomer, bent over and still coughing, and finally two stalwarts of the company: the massively glamorous Maria, *prima donna con molto brio*, whose operatic dimensions and high colouring earned her the approval of a thousand road-menders, and Bruno Retz, tall, slim and elegant but with broad shoulders and a virile neck, the apotheosis in appearance of what Rupert, openly, and Ed, secretly, would have wished for themselves.

Five personalities with but a single purpose this morning: to cover with Jane the movements needed for Act One of *Traviata*, *Violetta*'s ill-fated party at which she abandons her comfortable life as *Baron Douphol*'s mistress in favour of *Alfredo's* youthful passion, romantic no doubt, but sadly lacking in profit for a girl without resources, especially one already in the grip of a fatal disease.

The problem with most *Violettas* is that they look more likely to die of overeating than of tuberculosis. Isabelle, though generously curvaceous, had the slender arms and legs of a much younger woman, and George, watching her with the dispassionate eye of an impresario rather than the lustful one of a lover, was vain enough to congratulate himself on one part in his opera superlatively well cast.

Whether she could sing the part was quite another question!

Winston, his rich baritone given added depth by his bulk, was a little controversial as *Germont père*, given the likelihood of engaging a *white* man as his son *Alfredo*. But, and this was the crux with just one hundred and twenty hours to go, who was going to sing *Alfredo* anyway, black, white or just plain orange?

'Have you tried Gaspard?' said Maria helpfully, adjusting her bra.

'He's gone back to New Zealand,' chimed in Bruno.

'Well . . . ' she paused, 'what about dear Ted?'

'Dear Ted,' said George wearily, 'is doing something at the Albert Hall.'

'I *know!*' she shrieked. 'See? Your Maria always solves your problems!' She cast a withering look in the direction of Isabelle. '*Frangio!* There!'

George raised his eyes to the ceiling. 'Can't you remember his singing *Almaviva* to your *Rosina*? His top note?'

She giggled irrepressibly. 'Oh! That top note! It was. . . . ' she mused, '*impossIBile!*'

'These are important clients,' put in Isabelle, joining them. 'They could bring George lots of work.'

Maria shrugged. 'Every client is important. Which is why Maria always gives of her best.' And, with a luxurious roll of her hips, she stalked off to see what costumes Jane had managed to scrounge from her friend in the wardrobe department of the Brent Cross College of Opera and Drama.

'Poor Maria!' sighed Isabelle, with a gentle little smile. 'She needs a man. It must be hard to be old. . . . God! Will someone help me with this wig. I cannot get it to stay put.'

There was a burst of discordant sound from the piano, where old Mr Sumption, the redheaded session pianist hired by the hour for subsistence wages and a steady supply of Woodbines, was trying out his new spectacles.

'Back in position, please!' shouted Jane. 'We'll take it from the start again. One more time!'

By five thirty that evening, they were half-way through Act One, with Mr Sumption crooning *Alfredo*'s music from the piano to fill in the gaps.

As Bruno remarked, under his breath, to Winston, 'It's surprising how much quicker it is, when you're missing one of the two principal characters.'

The new *Marchese* had yet to be heard giving out a single audible note.

Chapter Thirteen

Wednesday evening found Solomon in strange company. Just in the lee of St Paul's Cathedral, on the river side, is a warren of narrow streets, a medieval labyrinth which must somehow have escaped destruction in the great fire which consumed the original Gothic cathedral of St Paul in 1666. These winding ways, some of them still cobbled, give access to a number of ancient inns, among them The Bishop's Pawn. This, an authentic hostelry of the sort most usually associated with Dickens, clung awkwardly to the steepest of these little slopes, its blackened timbers beetling half over the alleyway and its grimy windows seeming to promise dreadful villainy within.

Nor would these expectations have been much allayed by its only public room, an angular chamber with a slippery stone-flagged floor and heavy beamed ceiling, principally lit by damp coals that snarled and spat from the glowing grate.

'Another Black Velvet for my friend!' Solomon

was in celebration mode, his face lit up with artificial mirth. Next to him, hunched alongside the dusty bar lined with dirty glasses, sat a dwarf. He was, it was clear, unaccustomed to such convivial and generous hospitality. With his Mister Punch nose, all varicose veins, and his crooked shoulders, he looked like a ventriloquist's doll alongside his tall companion.

'You're a good friend, Reuben,' he said, with just the slightest hesitation in pronouncing his new friend's name. Not many people were kind to him, most preferring to avert their eyes from his gnarled and undergrown appearance. This man, by contrast, had made an instant friend of him, though they had only very recently met. The last thing he wanted to do was offend him by getting his name wrong!

'I love a good laugh,' said his tall companion with an infectious chuckle. 'I've got two tickets for that show at Victoria!'

'*Jolson?*' The little man was almost speechless with excitement.

'That's it! I thought we'd go there and then on to one of those little Italian restaurants where they have opera singers . . . ?'

'I'd love that,' said the dwarf, with eager simplicity. 'I really would.'

'Excellent!' said Solomon. 'And I want to ask your advice about playing a little prank on a friend of mine!' His eyes sparkled so brilliantly that his grey companion, a man of few pleasures, felt himself bubbling with a contagious glee.

'I hope I can help,' he said.

'I hope you can,' replied Solomon, his eyelids drooping over to disguise the gleam of triumph. 'Drink up, we'll miss the show!'

George, by contrast, spent the whole evening burrowing among his files, six drawerfuls of old papers, five hundred single sheets, each bearing the tawdry details of an opera singer's life:

Name: Sidney Edward Lupus
Born: 20 October 1961
Educ: 1972–1979
Eleanor Hibbert Comprehensive
6 GCSE (A–D)
A levels: Music A, Italian B, English E.
Piano Grade 7, Singing Grade 7
Viola Grade 6.
1979–1982
Royal Western College of Music
Finalist Susan Bisatt Prize.
Winner RWCM Special Prize.
Roles:

1980	Così Fan Tutte	Chorus	RWCM
1981	Billy Budd	Chorus	RWCM
1982	Fledermaus	Alfred	RWCM

1985	La Traviata	Chorus	Earls Ct
1986	Carmen	Chorus	Wembley
1989	Don Giovanni	Ottavio	Operamad
1995	Don Giovanni	Chorus	Operamad

Special skills: Martial arts, swimming.

What, wondered George, could have happened in 1989 that led to a six-year gap before Operamad, one of his less than glamorous rivals, could bring themselves to employ the man again, and even then only in their chorus?

In the fifteen years since he had left singing college, Lupus must have earned less than a thousand pounds from his chosen career. Unless in receipt of some splendid private income, he had probably been moonlighting in a day-job, earning a perfectly respectable living as a butcher, or barman, or even in court as a barrister. The dream persisted, however; hence these particulars, only recently sent to George along with the other fifty-odd aspiring opera managers around the country, and maybe even further afield.

Certainly there was nothing there to suggest that he would be able to delight a City audience in the cavernous Egyptian Hall of the Mansion House with his rendition of the major role of *Alfredo*. And his sheet was in no way different from a hundred others, a hundred hopeless tenors, destined to spend much of their lives yearning for the utterly impractical.

He put this, the last sheet in the pile, down with a sigh.

The telephone rang.

'Yes?'

'*Georges!*' There was the noise of heavy music in the background, and what sounded like geese.

'Isabelle?' She sounded pretty drunk.

'Do come, *chéri*! We're at The Dancing Dervish having such a wonderful time.'

'Who's we?' he asked, knowing the answer.

'Oh *Georges*! There's Alasdair, and his friend Lord . . . ' she had put her hand over the mouthpiece, ' . . . Lord Tabley who says you're his new best friend, and a woman who looks like a horse . . . ' There was shouting in the background, ' . . . *mais c'est vrai, Alasdair! Elle a le mien tout à fait d'un cheval! Mais un tel cheval . . . !* Alasdair says she doesn't look like a horse and that you know her too, she's the Lady Tabley. Anyway, we want you to join us.'

George stared at the clock opposite. 'It's nearly two in the morning!'

'All the better. You should be dancing with me here . . . ' more shouting ' . . . not making yourself tired with all those silly papers. I will find you an *Alfredo*. First we dance.' The line went dead.

By the time that George, unusually smart in his new silk dinner jacket, a recent present from Isabelle from the proceeds of subletting her Bayswater flat, arrived, The Dancing Dervish was fairly shuddering with sound. They were fortunate in being placed between a large warehouse on one side and a fire station on the other, with a small public park at the back. Otherwise the residents would surely have risen in a body and burned the place down, such was the thumping volume of its jungle beat.

Inside it was worse. He felt physically invaded by the music. It attacked his ears and made his jaw vibrate.

'Are you on your own?' A slender black brunette had detached herself from the bar and slipped her arm through his.

'I'm looking for some friends.'

'Come and find me if they're not here,' she said, shouting over the music, but still managing to suggest discreet but uninhibited allure.

For a moment she held his gaze, an eye contact promising unspeakable physical ecstasy, and turned away.

'There you are! We've got the table over there by the pillar!' George turned reluctantly to find himself next to Alasdair Rumbold, Isabelle's friend, admirer and would-be lover. 'Whisky do?'

'Thank you.' George tried painfully to disguise his dislike of the man. There was nothing palpably repulsive about him. He was a good height, dark-haired, with even features, a wide smile and a refreshing air of enthusiasm for whatever he happened to be doing. But, as a rival for Isabelle's body, he was doomed to be an enemy to George.

'Your sister's in sparkling form!' This was the problem. Since all the world accepted Isabelle as his half-sister, an uncomfortable concealed connection that they had only discovered well into their affair, nobody saw him as a rival, though they eyed her husband Winston, an almost totally innocent bystander, as the real threat. Consequently George had to try to dissemble his own very intense feelings as best he could.

'Good.' It was the best he could do.

'*Gary! My dear chap!*' Foghorn camaraderie from Lord Tabley.

'It's George,' said George politely.

'Absolutely! You haven't got a drink!'

'I'm getting him some whisky,' said Rumbold over his shoulder, elbowing his way towards the bar.

'Your sister's a *cracker*,' said the peer, winking ferociously. 'I gather she'll be singing the lead, er . . . La . . . well . . . whatever . . . ' His voice tailed away, momentarily at a loss.

George came to his rescue. '*Violetta*,' he said. After all, why should the man know. George knew nothing about interest rates or Swiss Franc put-options, if there were such things. Each to his own.

'You haven't met the wife?'

Isabelle was right. Lady Tabley looked exactly like a horse. She had a straggled fringe, a long lugubrious nose between two wide liquid brown eyes, an absolute barrage of splayed yellowing teeth and gangling legs. Strap a saddle on her and she'd probably whinny with delight. 'How do you do, Lady Tabley?'

'Oh, Ja-net, *please.*'

'It's very loud, isn't it?' He sat down beside her, trying not to meet Isabelle's satirical gaze for fear of giggling.

'Very.' She took a long swig from a glass full of ice. 'Yum!'

'Here we are.' Rumbold was back, with a similar glass that smelt deliciously of malt whisky. 'Just what the doctor ordered.'

'Thank you.' George was uncomfortably aware that he was drinking the best part of thirty pounds sterling.

'To Saturday!' said Lord Tabley.

'To Saturday,' exclaimed George, dutifully raising his glass.

'Saturday,' chimed in Isabelle. 'And all who sail in her. Oh dear! I think we've run out of champagne.'

'Don't worry!' Rumbold had hardly sat down, yet he was off again, jostling and shoving, Mister Perfect Host himself, his heart no doubt singing hosannas at the prospect of ramming Isabelle repeatedly into some convenient mattress, especially now that her grumpy brother had been persuaded to join the party.

92

George, watching him with a grim little smile, reflected that this was one of the great mysteries of the Universe: the immense heartache and energy expended on seducing one particular woman, in physical detail so little differentiated from a hundred others, while ten thousand alternatives lounged unnoticed all around. The little dark brunette, for example, would probably fuck Rumbold for fifty quid, and give him a wonderful time, expecting so very little in return, being grateful even for a little courtesy in the process. Yet he might spend ten thousand pounds or more pursuing Isabelle and then be no nearer her knickers than Timbuktu.

'What are you shaking your head at?' enquired Janet Tabley, showing her teeth.

'The human comedy,' said George, smiling wearily. 'It never fails to amaze me.'

'*Nowt so queer as folk!*' she said, with an unexpectedly understanding smile. 'I can see that you're very fond of your sister.'

He avoided her gaze, nodding with what he hoped was a convincing sincerity. 'Of course,' he said. 'She's all I've got.'

'She loves you very much.'

This was getting too personal. He stood up. 'Do you know where the ... er ... ?' What would she call the toilets? The 'little boys' room'?

'The lavatories? I think they're over there.' She pointed at a distant corner. 'At least, that's where

Prosper keeps going. I suppose it may be the back door of the den upstairs.' She laughed discordantly.

'Really?'

She giggled, and wiped her forehead. He suddenly realized that she was fairly drunk. 'You've never married?'

'Not yet.' How was he to escape this inquisition? 'Excuse me.'

'Go right ahead.'

'Thank you.' He started to force his way through the crowd, packed thick with mesmerized people, their eyes glazed with lust, alcohol or just plain exhaustion. 'Excuse me.' Three feet forward. 'Sorry.' Two feet back.

'So you found them!'

He looked down. It was the slender black girl, smiling up at him with amusement.

'Yes,' he said. 'I did.'

'Too bad,' she said. 'Another time, eh?'

'Another time.' On an impulse, he bent over and kissed her lips. She tasted of honey, and something bitter.

'Don't make it too long,' she said, and squeezed his trousers. As she turned away, she slipped a card into his hand. 'I'm expensive,' she said, 'but it's worth it. You can get a reference too.'

In the toilet he found Lord Tabley, urinating with patrician unconcern into the only washbasin.

'Bloody inconvenient,' said the peer, waggling his member.

'These look easier,' murmured George, heading for the intended receptacles.

'I'm sure you're right,' said the other, laboriously buttoning up his trousers. 'I need a drink.'

'Rehearsals are going well,' said George desperately.

'Good! Excellent!' Lord Tabley walked very slowly to the door and threw it open with a crash, alarming a small man on his way in. Left alone, George looked at his watch. Two thirty-six! Isabelle would be on for singing her big duet in eight hours time, except she had no opposite number as yet. Why had she dragged him here? Why weren't they tucked up peacefully in bed instead of drinking with all these ghastly people?

'*Fuck you!*' he shouted.

'Are you talking to me?' said the small man with a liquid grin. 'Because if so, you're on.'

George stared, then ran from the room.

Chapter Fourteen

Thursday the 22nd of November dawned raw and cold, though this was lost on George and Isabelle, both lying senseless next to, yet so far from, each other beneath their heavy duckdown duvet in his Hammersmith flat.

For Paul Dumeige, comfortably settled in a small hotel at the back of Knightsbridge, it was a time for busy telephoning and reading the early morning faxes from the Incident Room they had set up in the old police cells beneath the Mansion House courtroom.

'More coffee, sir?' The waiter hovered, impressed and interested in the immaculate Frenchman.

'Thank you.' The man's interest was not reciprocated, so he retreated to the kitchen to pour himself another shot of vodka. Serving breakfast at seven every morning to good-looking rich bastards who ignored him was not how he had envisaged his life. However, at forty-eight, that was how it looked like staying. He drank the vodka in one gulp, and then, despite himself, poured out some more.

Commander Bright lived with his wife in a small Georgian street off Barnes Common. For all their neighbours knew, theirs was an idyllic marriage: no mortgage, two cats, and his-and-hers red Honda Accords.

'Do you want a cup of tea?'

'Who?' Mrs Bright smiled vacantly and dropped her plastic plate on the floor for the third time. Alzheimer's at fifty-two. It was hard on her, thought Bright, watching her struggle to remember who he was, but a damn sight harder on him.

At least he had a mistress round the corner in Breadshaw Street, a pouty little waitress with two illegitimate daughters whose wardrobe he gladly subsidized in return for sexual access to her plump body. Covertly he glanced at his watch. There should just be time to pop in on her before his car came to collect him.

'Going to see your tart?' enquired Mrs Bright with a lopsided smile. God, but she was unpredictable!

'No,' he said patiently. 'Just going to get some cigarettes. Back in a trice!'

'Take your time. I'm not going anywhere.' That at least was true.

The Tableys, like George and Isabelle, were still asleep, though in separate bedrooms, in their five-storey Chelsea mansion in The Vale, and would remain so until called with tea at eight by their octogenarian housekeeper. Alasdair Rumbold, however, had already been up for two hours.

A toiler at the coalface of capitalism, as a prosecuting counsel employed by the Treasury at the Old Bailey, Alasdair rose every morning at five, showered, shaved, and was drinking his first cup of decaffeinated espresso as he scanned the current briefs before climbing into the Chambers car, complete with driver, which arrived punctually every morning on the doorstep of his Camden Town mews house.

He was lucky in that he had never needed much sleep, and that his obsessive search for wealth had led him to one of the two or three busiest Treasury Chambers in London.

On this particular morning Alasdair's movements were a trifle lethargic, appropriate for a man who had spent several hours and many hundreds of pounds in the pursuit of one particular female's good opinion.

'No matter!' His mouth formed the words as he swapped channels to catch the CNN headlines. Yet it did matter. Very much. Isabelle, with her creamy complexion, serpentine curves and entrancing soft voice, was everything he had ever desired in a woman. To think of her married to that gross black barrel of lard, called *of all names* Winston, was more than he could really bear. He punched the keys of his portable notebook computer, stabbing repeatedly at the space key as if it could transmit some lethal dose directly into Winston's veins. What excesses would the computer have experienced could he have seen Isabelle as she really was, her sleeping face lying flushed beside that of *George*, the man who had just drunk one hundred and twenty pounds worth of malt whisky at Alasdair's expense?

Swallowing the scalding coffee, he dragged on his jacket, scooped up the ribboned files and the hat and overcoat that hung ready on the chair by the door, and hurried out into the misty street. Twenty minutes now separated him from his Chambers; twenty minutes when some new approach, some new line of cross-examination might suggest itself in his constant search for success.

Born into comparative luxury, his mother, a City solicitor, had sent him to Radley, and he had earned his own entry to Keble College, Oxford, thanks to his muscular rowing. Now it was up to him. With Dad in long-term care and his mother long dead, he was the bread winner for a family which currently consisted of one able-bodied male and one chronic invalid. But how he wished to extend the family, to include an able-bodied female, and, through a delicious and regular interaction between the two of them, a positive sprawl of tiny gurgling Rumbolds!

As for poor Winston, unwitting recipient of Alasdair Rumbold's jealous spleen? He too was curled up in bed, dead to the world and with no intention of waking before his radio unleashed the latest Classic FM motoring news at 08.55 a.m. in time for him to rise, bathe and reach the *Traviata* rehearsals in Fulham by 10.29 a.m.

And it *was* true, he *was* lying with one massive hand cupping the warm breast of a satisfied woman, his own desires comprehensively disarmed by the previous night's exertions. But this woman was not his wife Isabelle. She was, instead, a casual pick-up, a winsome creature of at least forty-five who had responded to his roving wink as they travelled opposite each other on the Circle Line the previous evening, and who even now was staring cross-eyed at his ceiling, and wondering if she dared ask him for proof of Aids-free status.

In the Mansion House, by contrast, few people slept. Threlfall himself, increasingly uneasy at the unaccustomed security around him and the threat that instigated it, was lying in the State bed which had lulled a hundred Lord Mayors night after night, banquet after banquet, during their once-in-a-lifetime year of overeating and Civic self-satisfaction.

He was a man who had made many enemies in the course of a long career on either side of the divide between sharp practice and fraud. Other people's opinions had never mattered to him, except when they were in a position to assist him, a process which his benefactors usually came to regret. But the name Solomon had no resonance for him.

What he did know, however, and what he did not want to discuss with the police (hence his reticence that first day with Bright and Dumeige) was the connection between himself, Hopkirk, von Arnim and Tait. In the summer of 1963, with the Macmillan administration clearly dying on its feet, Hopkirk and he had formed a small private bank with its share-holding registered through a dummy board in the Bahamas headed by von Arnim. Its strategy was simple. It bought up heavily discounted debt from the more respectable, that is the more squeamish, High Street banks and then took aggressive action either to acquire majority stakes in the companies concerned prior to liquidating them or, in the case of individuals, bullying them into bankruptcy, with Tait, then an ambitious young accountant, put in as receiver.

There was nothing innately illegal about this operation except in so far as the Bahamian base enabled Threlfall, Tait and Hopkirk, all UK residents, to evade the very heavy taxation introduced by the Wilson Government in the years following 1964 as well as the exchange control restrictions. What had been much more controversial had been Tait's heavy-armed tactics. There had been at least two suicides. Threlfall stared up at the patterned silk canopy of his bed. Now why had he been thinking of one of them recently, the man whose company had specialized in tapestries? And there had been a child. It was dark still, for the windows were concealed behind matching vermilion silk curtains. Surely he had suddenly been reminded of that. Quite recently. Without realizing it, he drifted back into sleep.

In the blue corridor beyond the Boudoir, DS Tatham could have done with some sleep himself. He'd been on duty since midnight. But he knew there were three more Special Branch men round the building, especially DCI Jameson who was not known to be sympathetic to his men who dozed off on duty. He wondered how DS Rogers was doing round the corner at the top of the service stairs. The worst of these damn video cameras – there was one gazing at him now – was you never had a chance of a fag, not that that was permitted at all in this great barn of a building. The door opposite him opened, and two young men in shirt-sleeves came through.

'Morning, mate!' It was two of the footmen, Frederick and Peter judging by the list of named photos he'd spent the whole weekend memorizing. They were on their way down to the pantry to get ready for the day's events, notably a ceremonial lunch, before preparing both the Lord Mayor and the Lady Mayoress's breakfast trays. All right for some! He growled a greeting and made a note in his duty ledger, noting the time: 06.11 a.m. Then he rose and went back to pacing backwards and forwards, between the top of the two main staircases. At least he had that welcome weight, his Fletcher and Houston .38 Standard-Grip revolver, strapped under his right armpit in case Solomon should chance to call.

On the top floor, Gwladys and Dorothy were just stirring. Lifelong friends, they could hardly have been more different to look at. Gwladys was tall and starched, with a jutting jaw, silver-grey hair and a few whiskers straggling about the chin. She spoke rarely but with authority, in a deep slow voice.

Dorothy, by contrast, was tiny. Round as a squashball, with tight curls dyed a vividly uncon-vincing orange, she chattered and giggled in a kind of demented squeak, accompanied by harsh cackles of genuine laughter that ended alarmingly on a high note of rising hysteria.

They had come as a package, at the end of the Eighties, and had been there ever since, working hard and causing a certain amount of discreet amusement among the otherwise wholly male household.

Just one man and one woman slumbered on peacefully under that broad eighteenth-century roof: Jerry had stopped over on a camp-bed in the 'Lord Mayor's dressing room', ostensibly to double-check their computer security but in reality to protect his own carefully plotted plans, and Susan Threlfall herself, lying toes-up on her bed next to the two tall pedimented windows that faced the Bank of England across the street.

Jerry's sleep was entirely natural, the fortunate gift of a healthy digestion; Mrs Threlfall's was chemically induced, the stupor of a pint and a third of Gordon's, helped on its way with tonic, bitter lemon, pure orange juice and anything else she could tip into a glass of honest gin to disguise the taste of the one liquid on earth that could still bring her peace.

Chapter Fifteen

That same morning, George's alarm began a stealthy beeping at 09.40 a.m. As this had no effect, at 09.45 this gradually grew in volume until the whole room resonated with an electronic howl.

'*George!*'

'What?' He rolled over and hid his head under a pillow.

'Are you *deaf?*'

'Who?'

She shook her head angrily. 'I'm not joking. Stop that noise. *C'est affreux. Vraiment, vite!*'

He reached out an awkward arm and, after a long time fumbling, the alarm was silenced. 'Tea?'

'*Tea?*' she mimicked, and turned over in the bed away from him. 'Tea!'

'I love you,' he said, eyeing her narrow backbone and swelling buttocks with uncontrollable excitement.

There was a long oppressive silence, and then she spoke. '*Coffee,*' she said. 'Coffee is what people drink in the morning. In Paris, in Rome, in Berlin, in Vienna, even in St Petersburg, the *mondaine* drink coffee. I have to find myself in bed with a man whose first words in the morning are *"Tea?"*!!'

He stroked her spine. 'You are beautiful. Would you like some coffee?'

She turned towards him, a smile gleaming in her wide blue eyes. 'I am beautiful?'

'*Very* beautiful!'

'*C'est vrai.*' She curled herself against him. 'I am lucky.'

'We have exactly forty-one minutes until rehearsals,' he said, taut with desire, and turned away to conceal his embarrassment.

She frowned. 'You sound tense. Let your little sister *assist*—'

'I'll get the bloody coffee!' he said, in a stifled tone, and reaching out, he wrapped himself in last night's discarded towel.

Shrugging, she leapt off the bed. 'I'll run the bath.'

It was ten twenty-six when George parked the *deux-chevaux* smartly beside Ed's battered Ford.

'Why are you still frowning? Life is good: the trees, the flowers, we are young!'

George shrugged. 'What do you expect? We have no *Alfredo*.'

Isabelle nodded. Thursday to Saturday left just three days to rehearse and then perform a complicated opera. Even someone who knew the part would have difficulty.

'Shall I let Rupert try?' he asked while locking his car.

'You do and I leave. *Je m'en vais, now!*' She set her face in a ferocious *moue*. There were limits. And Rupert Brock singing *Alfredo* to her *Violetta* with Alasdair in the audience was way beyond her limits, even for George.

'Listen.'

'I *am* listening, *chéri!*'

'No!' He took her hand to pacify her. 'I mean: *listen.*'

Above the rattle and hum of the Fulham Broadway traffic could be heard a voice raised in song:

> ' . . . *cool gales shall fan the breeze.*
> *Trees for-or a . . . *'
> 'Who's that?'
> ' . . . *shall crowd into a gla-a-ade . . . *'
> 'Search me.'
> ' . . . *into a gla-a-ade . . . *'
> 'He can sing.'
> ' . . . *into a gla-a-ade . . . *'

'You're right. It's a tenor and he sounds like poncing Peter Pears. But he *can* sing!'

'So what are you waiting for?' she asked. The sound was coming not from the church hall where they rehearsed, but from the church itself, a mean strangulated essay in suffering, suffering in this case piled on with modern concrete and prestressed imagination-free angularity.

George, oblivious to all but the voice, ran to the swing doors, pushed his way through them and strode into the body of the church.

A man was accompanying himself on the harmonium, peering short-sightedly at the music propped against the stand.

'Excuse me.'

The man jumped. 'Hello?' He'd knocked the music to the ground, and scrabbled about picking up the various sheets.

'I'm George Sinclair.' He put out his hand which the other man took. It was impossible to ignore the brash scarlet crossed-ribbon device adorning the lapel of his perfectly-tailored twill jacket. Aids-awareness! Who isn't, thought George, now they force it down our throats?

'I'm Gerard Combe,' said the man.

'Nice to meet you.'

'And you. Are you the Vicar?'

'No. I'm with the opera company rehearsing in the church hall.'

'What fun!'

George smiled. 'Sometimes. Do you sing opera?'

The man shuffled his feet. 'I've always *wanted* to. My teacher says I should wait.'

'Teachers are notoriously overcautious.'

'Do you sing too?'

'I play the piano,' said George.

'Oh?'

'Actually,' said George, mentally going for gold, 'I'm looking for someone to sing *Alfredo* at the moment.'

'Really?'

'Yes,' said George, praying for patience. 'On Saturday.'

'*Alfredo*?' The man stared. He was tallish, with blond hair, long dark eyelashes, and opaque, greyish, eyes. 'On Saturday? As in the day after *tomorrow*?'

We have Mastermind here, thought George, Mister Mensa *himself*, but he kept his smile warm. 'I could coach whoever did it every evening,' he said.

'Do you pay?'

'Of course!'

'How much?' The man seemed suddenly more real, more present. 'It *is* my favourite part. I sing along with Pavarotti, so I do know it.'

George bit his lip. To lose this heaven-sent man now would be madness. 'Three hundred pounds,' he said, 'seeing as it's such short notice. But don't tell the others! They'd murder me.'

The man considered. 'God! It's worth a punt,' he said. 'I'll do it!'

'Great! Come next door and meet the team.'
George led him across the car-park, his mind much
exercised by wondering whether the man would
have agreed to do it for two hundred after all.

Chapter Sixteen

By that same Thursday morning, all Jerry's arrangements for flight were in place. The Lord Mayor
himself was beginning to shrink with the strain. No
mere optical illusion, Threlfall's shirt-collar, instead
of appearing to be trying to asphyxiate its occupant,
hung loose and comfortable round that doughty
dewlap.

'You look awful,' said Jerry cosily.

'So do you,' snapped back his employer. 'Don't
you have one good suit? I'm ashamed to admit you
work for me.'

'Not as ashamed as I'd be if I had to name you
as my employer at the Old Bailey,' came the surpris-
ingly acid reply.

Threlfall stared. 'It's too late for us to start falling
out now,' he said quietly. 'We've both done well out
of our partnership.'

Jerry nodded, comfortably aware that within
twenty-four hours he would have scooped the
rewards of both of them, treasure beyond anything

he had ever coveted as a scholarship pupil at Winchester, only twenty years before. He had put his brain to profitable endeavour, if not with ethical success. Manners makyth Man, perhaps, but money makyth men like him.

He tapped a few more keys. 'No time spent in reconnaissance is ever wasted.' That had been his old headmaster's favourite dictum. And it had been proved right in this case. The long hours Jerry had spent laboriously learning to programme computers had given him this, in the end, decisive advantage over Threlfall. By the time his departure was noticed, this whole system would have been so comprehensively scrambled that no one would ever be able to sort the thing out, least of all the Lord Mayor.

Almost as an entertainment for himself, he had spent the last thirty-six hours reworking the BAK files so that every tempting trail led into a morass of indecipherable detail. People could, and probably would, spend months, even years, trying to make sense out of his chaos, but he would be safe and rich in South America, and Threlfall would be in gaol or, even better, dead!

He looked at his watch.

'Why do you keep doing that?'

'I've got an appointment with Mrs Clench.'

'Who's she?'

'Possible recruit to deal with the EDT account problems.'

'Well, you'd better go and meet her. I can't be worrying about that as well as all this bloody nonsense.'

'You think it is nonsense?' enquired Jerry maliciously.

Threlfall growled angrily. 'Of course it is.'

'I never was quite sure how you and Hopkirk fitted in.'

'Then there's no need for you to speculate about it now, is there?' snapped his employer.

'Wasn't Tait the man behind that repossession scandal?'

The Lord Mayor stood up. '*Jerry.*'

'Yes?'

'Go to your appointment. *Now.*'

'Very good, Lord Mayor.'

Jerry, delighted, hurried from the room without a backward glance, listening to the door being double-locked behind him without the slightest feeling of regret or sympathy for the man he was abandoning. He was taking nothing with him. What he needed had been sent ahead electronically, the Internet having scooped the postal system for both speed and ease of passage.

He had two goodbyes to make, his mother in Harpenden and a young man who worked by day in the Harrow branch of Sainsbury's.

It was on his way back from the latter, some two

hours later, that he felt the familiar vibration of the mobile phone he carried in his jacket pocket.

'Tomkins.'

'Mr Tomkins? Is that you?' It was Brigadier Gooch, his voice anxious, frightened even.

'Brigadier?' They'd hardly been on speaking terms, let alone telephoning.

'Something dreadful's happened.'

Jerry stopped. 'What?'

'It's the Lord Mayor. He's been killed!'

'*What?*' For all the threats and security measures, Jerry had never really believed in it all.

'He insisted on leaving the building. I told him not to!' The Brigadier sounded distraught. 'He'd had a call from your airline.'

Jerry felt sweat suddenly dripping down his arm. '*Airline?*'

'Yes. What?' Jerry heard muttering in the background. 'Commander Bright wants you to identify the body. They've taken it to the mortuary at St Paul's Graveyard. Number One. Can you then come back to the Mansion House?'

'Of course.' He was quite tempted to take the underground straight to Heathrow, but that was too great a risk. If Threlfall knew about his flight, others might too. Better, he decided swiftly, to play along with the authorities, heaping any blame on to the dead man. Dead! To his surprise, he found himself mourning the gross embezzler who had worked him so hard. At least the man had paid him generously. And there'd been a certain buccaneering bravado about the way he operated that had appealed to Jerry's more cautious spirit.

It only took him twenty minutes to make his way to the mortuary, a low humourless building built of chunks of dank grey stone.

It was drizzling now, but he hardly noticed as he climbed the steps leading through the fat municipal pillars and pushed his way through the glass doors into the hall.

The hunched attendant looked up from his ledger.

'Mr Tomkins?'

'That's me,' said Jerry cautiously.

'You've come to identify a body?'

Jerry nodded, at a momentary loss for words. *Threlfall!* So large a man, in girth, ambition and in criminal expertise. To end like this! It seemed, somehow, unreal. 'Reginald Threlfall,' he said. 'The Lord Mayor of London.'

The attendant nodded his head and twinkled at him. He was, after all, used to illustrious corpses, here, in the lee of the great cathedral. 'So I believe.' He led the way into a neat rectangular waiting room, with powder blue sofas and a large empty ashtray on a low deal table. 'They say you shouldn't smoke, but I shan't notice,' he said obligingly.

Jerry shook his head. 'I'd better see him,' he said grimly. After all, he still had a plane to catch, though it would surely have to be delayed for a day or two.

'Through here, sir.' It must be weird, Jerry thought, working among dead bodies, washing them, showing them, the only man alive among the recent dead. 'This way.' The man ushered him through a metal door into an icy atmosphere. The whole room seemed lined in metal and there was a distinct haze in the air, as if they were trekking through Antarctica. 'I'll leave you alone.'

'Which . . . ?' There were perhaps twenty bodies in all, laid out individually under nylon sheets on hospital trolleys.

'Over there . . . by the light . . . ' The little man's voice sounded very distant, as if he was already closing the door.

Jerry trod awkwardly over towards the trolley indicated. It was very cold, and, he felt, very intimidating. The corpse was immense and pulling back the sheet, he could scarcely suppress a cry of alarm. The face, grey and immobile, was that of a *complete stranger*.

'B . . but . . . ' His jaw was shaking with consternation. This wasn't Threlfall, or anything like him. He moved to the next corpse and pulled off the sheet. A woman, dreadfully mutilated. And the next, a young man, seemingly untouched, and all of them that same grey, with that same clay-like solidity, as if they'd been modelled in dirty wax.

'. . . *croc*' *é délizia . . . délizi' al cor . . .* ' Less of a voice than a hoarse whisper.

Jerry's whole scalp shifted with a frozen shivering sensation. So it did happen in real life, all the hairs *could* rise at the back of his neck.

'*Oh-oh . . . Je-erry!*'

'No!' he whispered. 'No!'

'*No?*' enquired the whisper. '*No?*'

Jerry swung round, searching for the source of this terrifying sound. 'Where are you?' He was searching for a weapon, but his hands were sweating. 'Who . . . ?'

The whisper chuckled. '*You know who, don't you, Jerry? You followed me, didn't you? That was clever.*'

'What do you want?' Jerry's voice rose to a scream as he blundered against a trolley without seeing a corpse at the far end of the room behind him rise noiselessly from where it lay and started padding towards him, the bare feet soundless on the linoleum.

'*Jerry!*' The whisper was right in his ear.

He turned to face the man he expected. 'I mean you no harm. I did you no harm.'

'I know,' said Solomon in his normal voice. 'You're planning to run out on him, aren't you? Flight BA4293, yes?' Jerry gasped. 'But you know who I

117

am. I can't allow that, now can I? Did you like my impression of Dick Gooch?'

'I can give you money. Please,' said Jerry. Tears were running down his face. He seemed to have aged ten years. *'God!'* he suddenly screamed. 'What's that?'

'This?' Solomon gave a dreadful little smile. 'Just a knife.' It must have been two foot long at least, and was very thin, more like a needle.

'But . . . '

'If you stay still, it'll be so much easier.'

'You don't have to kill me. I'll do what you want. I'll tell the police everything!' He was slipping on the floor, his legs shaking and shivering in his panic. 'About them, I mean.'

'You don't understand, do you?' Solomon's eyes glittered in the half-light. 'I actually *enjoy* killing.' And lunging forward, he thrust the blade, again and again, deep into Jerry's agonized chest, never stopping even when the little man had slipped backwards on to the floor, but continuing to strike until his hand and arm, rising and falling, were sticky with blood. 'Aah!' It was a soft obscene sigh of pleasure, and relief. 'That's *much* better.' There was blood everywhere, thick red gobbets. The murderer wiped his dripping lips, and sighed luxuriously.

As he was entirely naked, he rubbed himself down vigorously with the nylon sheet that had covered him and then re-donned the white surgical surcoat that he had hung across one of the other bodies. He heard footsteps outside, so hurried to the door just as the bent little attendant opened it.

'All right, mate?'

'Yes, thank you,' said Solomon smiling.

'Thank *you*,' said the gnome, grinning happily up at his friend. 'I like a good laugh too. Did your friend enjoy the joke?'

'He certainly did.'

'It must have scared him!'

'Mmm. Perhaps.'

'Where is he?'

'Over there.'

The attendant shuffled curiously into the room, and the man who called himself Solomon slipped his arm round his chest from behind and neatly slit his throat, precipitating a further brief burst of blood on to the slippery floor. It was all so easy. This time he merely gave a little grunt of satisfaction, a job well done, and lowered his victim tenderly on to the floor. He had no grudge against him. Quite the contrary. He had grown to like the bent little man, who had merely been in the right place at the right time, and who had served his purpose perfectly. Now it was time to get back to his preparations for Reginald Threlfall.

Chapter Seventeen

The discovery later that day, and subsequent identi-
fication, of Jerry's body caused panic in the Mansion
House.

At first Bright wouldn't believe it.

'What time did he leave the building?' he
demanded of DCI Jameson, a sturdy young man
with sparse red hair.

'Eleven-thirty-two. The Porter clocked him out
via the Walbrook entrance.'

'Why did no one tell me?'

Jameson met his chief's gaze impassively.
'Tomkins was in and out of the building all the time.
He only slept here last night because', he consulted
his notes, 'he told the Lord Mayor he had a major
job to finish on the computer.'

'I want that instrument impounded.'

'I tried that. Threlfall wouldn't even let me into
the room to look at it.'

'He'll have to change his tune now,' snapped
Bright. 'This is a murder inquiry.'

Jameson pursed his lips. 'You'll need a Court Order. I can tell you *that*. I don't know what he keeps in that room, but he's paranoid about locking and unlocking it.'

'What in God's name was Tomkins doing in a *mortuary*? Can anyone answer me that? Who was the other man again?'

'Richard Alan Pope. He's worked there twenty years as Deputy-Registrar.'

'Was there no one else in the building?'

Jameson nodded. 'That's the interesting part. It should have been closed today. The other staff were not due in until tomorrow morning. There's another mortuary at Bart's. The two sites work in tandem.'

'It's a puzzle.'

'Forensic say whoever did it will be covered in blood.'

'*Whoever did it!* We know who bloody did it. Mister Clever-Clogs himself.'

Jameson smiled grimly. 'He'll not get past my men.'

'He'd better not. Meanwhile I'm going to take charge of that computer.'

Elsewhere in the building, another tense meeting was discreetly in progress. The Corporation maintains four ceremonial officers to attend the Lord Mayor: the City Marshal, resplendent in red and gold frogging; the Mace-Bearer who, dressed in black robes topped off with a long Parliamentary wig, carries the Mace; the Sword-Bearer, who carries the Sword and wears a fur hat of positively Cossack solidity; and the Private Secretary, who bears the burden of making it all happen smoothly but isn't allowed to put on anything fancier than a morning tailcoat. Three of these men, Brigadiers Gooch, the Private Secretary, and Popham, the City Marshal, and Colonel Lumsden, the Sword-Bearer, had one thing in common: all three sported splendid Service moustaches, long since grown white in the course of time and duty. As a consequence of this, they were known within the building as 'The Three Walruses'. Nor was this necessarily a term of endearment. Walruses are famed for their aggression. The fourth officer, Captain Bennett, the Mace-Bearer, had no moustache and was on extended sick-leave, being in any case much looked-down-on as being of *naval* extraction.

'What do we do?' Gooch spread his hands on the table and the other two men bristled angrily at each other.

'The scandal will be very damaging,' said Popham.

'Those bastards at Westminster will use it against us,' added Lumsden. 'That at least is certain.'

In the internecine world of competition between Councils, few realize the bitterness of the struggle for municipal ascendancy. For centuries the City of London had boasted the only *Lord* Mayor. Then, that pass having been sold up north, they had at least managed to restrict the other upstarts to distant provinces of risible insignificance, maintaining their man's uniqueness within London. Then, twenty years ago, Westminster had sneaked through into parity. And the worst of it was, they had achieved this by recruiting one of the Walruses' erstwhile colleagues, one of their own kind, a City of London turncoat who had joined, and thereafter advanced, the cause of the enemy.

What was worse, the immemorial right of *The* Lord Mayor, that is, their Lord Mayor, to be given a hereditary baronetcy was lost for good at about the same time. By the time someone had appointed a Lord Mayor of *Neasden*, there'd be no point in being Lord Mayor at all.

'You're sure about this?' Popham raised his fine silver eyebrows. 'I mean, it's not another balls-up?'

'Why else would he keep the thing locked away like the Crown Jewels?'

'It's a huge jump from that to our needing to spy on our own Lord Mayor.' Popham looked round anxiously. 'Are we being observed by one of their bloody video things? They give me the creeps.'

Gooch chuckled. 'Not likely!'

'So what do we do?'

'I think,' said Gooch, 'that I'm going to try to

get hold of that computer myself and check there's nothing that could embarrass the Corporation or the other Aldermen. If I could wipe that before the stuff gets into the public domain, I suppose we could face the rest.'

'Do you know anything about computers?' asked Lumsden, impressed.

'A little,' came the acid rejoinder, 'since I'm a director of three software companies.'

'Dick's got his finger in a number of pies,' said Popham. 'That's why he's got a villa in Sardinia while I spend my holidays in Bournemouth!'

'I don't believe you've been to Bournemouth in your life!' At least Gooch was relaxed enough to smile. 'But how am I to get into that room without the Lord Mayor knowing?'

'Or the police!'

'The police don't matter,' said Gooch. 'They won't think it strange that I'm going in or out of anywhere. The big question is whether it's the sort of program I'm used to. If you are both in agreement, I'll try tonight, during the Banquet.'

Chapter Eighteen

The mirror opposite Threlfall shattered. He picked up another heavy tumbler and threw it at the same point, sending another shower of glass on to the floor. Immediately someone started hammering on the outer door.

'What do you want?'

'Lord Mayor? Lord Mayor?'

'What do you want?'

'Are you all right, sir?'

'Is that you, Frederick?'

The panic-stricken footman started hammering again. 'I've got two policemen here. Let us in!'

'Go *away*!' shouted Threlfall, his face contorted. 'I'm perfectly all right. I just want to be left alone, do you hear me? Otherwise I'll never be ready for the fucking Goldsmiths.'

The hammering stopped. He walked over to the pile of debris and kicked at it. Then, raising his head, he examined his appearance in what was left of the looking-glass.

'You've changed,' he said sourly, after a few minutes' contemplation. The face he had once known was all blotched and spread. Surely his parents would never recognize now this bloated many-coloured face which spoke of self-indulgence. Was there something cruel in those lips? He'd used to hope it was *diablerie*, not that it had ever helped him with women. What he'd had he'd had to pay for, apart from his wife. He seized the battered mirror and wrenched it off the wall. His wife! What use was she to him now? To hell with her, and her fine connections. He'd made his own way, he and Jerry. His mind halted abruptly.

Jerry was dead! And with him, or so it seemed, his access to the millions he had accumulated. His own accustomed password into the computer had yielded nothing but rubbish, and half the files seemed to have disappeared off the backup facility Jerry had once explained to him.

What if this Solomon did get to him? Jerry's death made it all suddenly very close indeed. What on earth had he been doing in a *mortuary*? Unexpectedly, he heard himself chuckling.

Threlfall crossed to the desk and picked up the whisky bottle. It was already half-empty. He pulled out the cork and threw it over his shoulder before raising the bottle to his lips. 'Fuck them all,' he muttered after taking a long pull. It hadn't helped. In fact he felt worse. Blearily, he reached out to steady himself against the fireplace. At least he'd made some preparations to defend himself. He could see that the police were no use at all. What he needed now was more food.

The hammering on the door started again.

'*Go away!*'

'It's Commander Bright, Lord Mayor. We need to speak.'

'I'm not speaking to anyone,' shouted Threlfall. 'I've got work to do.'

'Please let me in,' said Bright firmly. 'We've really got to discuss what's happened.' He had even taken the precaution of obtaining a Court Order, freshly delivered by motorcycle from a judge's chambers at the Old Bailey and now sticking awkwardly out of his jacket pocket . . .

'Later,' said Threlfall in a slurred voice. 'I'm going to have a bath.' And he resolutely kept silent until the policeman, faced with defeat or having to break the door down, reluctantly accepted the former and walked back down to his office.

'No good?' Dumeige was back, and scanning the notes made by the men on night duty.

'Drunk as a skunk!'

Dumeige smiled. 'I'm not sure I blame him. Any leads from the two bodies?'

'Nothing we couldn't have guessed for ourselves.'

'There must be something. Why don't you get Briggs' team to run through all telephone calls to and from the Mansion House over the last week. Tomkins must have had some reason to be in that mortuary.'

'You think Solomon lured him out of the house on purpose?' Bright examined the idea. 'I can see that, but why?'

Dumeige shrugged. 'Perhaps he saw Tomkins as a threat to his plan.'

'Or,' said Bright, raising his eyebrows, 'maybe Tomkins knew who he was!'

'An accomplice even.' Dumeige seemed less taken with this idea.

'It's worth checking. We still haven't established any connection between his four victims except that Threlfall is on the Board of Covent Garden and von Arnim was something to do with some appeal for renovating Stuttgart Opera House.'

'So?'

'So we wait.' Bright yawned and stretched.

'Wait?'

'Today's Thursday. He's given himself until midnight on Sunday. Seventy-two hours. He'll have to try. Then we'll have him.'

'What if he retreats? Waits for a better chance?'

Bright shook his head. 'He's done too well so far. He'll be thinking himself untouchable. The Napoleon syndrome. He'll try.'

'One thing,' said Dumeige, 'is that, by containing the Lord Mayor, you've succeeded in making him fight on your territory. Are there floor plans of this house?'

'Here.' Together the two men pored over the photostats.

'Looks good,' said Dumeige after careful scrutiny. 'My money's on Saturday night.'

'The opera?'

'Sure to be. Maximum strangers in the building, maximum capacity for confusion. It's his best chance.'

'Should we cancel?'

Dumeige frowned. 'No! That could give him an excuse to draw back. But make sure I have a chance to check everyone coming on our Lyon computer as well as yours. This man could be any nationality. And we know he's an accomplished impersonator.'

'In fact,' said Bright slowly, 'he might be a professional actor.'

The two men stared at each other. 'Or an opera singer, you mean?'

'Anything's possible. Perhaps that's the connection,' said the policeman, suddenly excited. 'Threlfall's a director of Covent Garden. Didn't Hopkirk's secretary say there was opera playing when he found the body?' He lifted a receiver. 'I'm going to follow this up.'

There was a discreet tap on the door. 'Now what?'

'It's Brigadier Gooch,' said DCI Jameson, putting his head round the door. 'Apparently the Lord Mayor will not be attending the Banquet tonight after all. He says he's too tired. The Private Secretary,' he gestured with his head to indicate the old soldier was still outside, 'seems very put out about it. But I said there was nothing you could do about it.'

'Anything I can do to help?' enquired Dumeige.

'Yes,' said Bright. 'You can find out some more about this so-called opera company!'

Chapter Nineteen

Happily unaware of all this drama concerning themselves, those who comprised the old guard of the
Floria Tosca Grand Opera Company spent Friday
hard at work on the last Act of *Traviata*, having
decided to leave the second Act for Saturday
morning to allow Gerard, the last-minute *Alfredo*,
another evening to learn his big part in that. There
wasn't even going to be time for a dress rehearsal.
But, as George kept telling himself, seven thousand
pounds was seven thousand pounds, a big induce-
ment to face an evening of professional shame.

The advantage of concentrating on the finale was
that those not appearing in the last Act, Maria,
Bruno, Rupert and the hunched and still silent
Henry, could spend a quiet day studying their music
with Mr Sumption accompanying them on the old
Vestry honky-tonk, while the two married couples,
Isabelle and Winston, Jane and Ed, concentrated on
getting Gerard sorted out in the finale while a
brooding George hammered away on the keyboard.

Whatever might be said about their performances, the company's rehearsals definitively lacked
spectator appeal.

'Can we have that again?'

'*Oh no!*' Isabelle turned away in despair. They'd
done it thirty-three times already. 'For God's sake
Winston! Just do what she says, can't you? This wig
is killing me.'

Winston's habitual good humour was beginning
to fray under his wife's relentless impatience. He
walked up to her, towering over her slight frame,
and laid one large menacing hand on her shoulder.
'I'm trying to,' he said, in a controlled quiet tone.
'But it's hard. I'm *Alfredo*'s father, right? I come in
and find you dying. You say, "Now I can die in
peace," and I say "*Che mai dite? Oh cielo! È ver!*' "

'*What are you saying? Oh God! It's true,*' intoned
Jane with elaborate patience.

'I *know* that,' snapped Winston. 'I speak Italian,
which is more than you do.'

'There's no need for that,' said Ed truculently.
This was the man he'd once caught actually engaged
in making love with Jane. He'd come to like him as
a friend, but, as Jane's husband, it still rankled.

'Please,' said Isabelle. 'Will someone do something about this wig?'

'Here!' said Jane impatiently, pulling a hat pin
from her sleeve. 'Stick this in it, and then shut up!'

'Remind me,' said George, wearily standing up

and coming over from the piano, 'what the problem is. I mean, we've got all of twenty-four hours before the show and one act still to do. I mean, there's certainly no *rush*.'

'The prob-lem,' said Jane, very slowly, 'i-s that since you have entrusted the production of this piece to *me*, and since we have three *days* to rehearse an opera that would normally need three *weeks* at least, it would help if the singers would make the few moves, the *very few* moves that I ask of them, *the first fucking time* and not the *fortieth*!' Her voice had risen to an angry squeak, and Winston had to turn away to hide a smile. '*There you are!*' she shouted triumphantly. 'That's *exactly* it.'

They stared at her. 'What?'

'That's the move I've been begging Winston to do for half an hour. He comes in, she tells him he's dying, he *turns away*.'

Winston shook his head. 'I just don't see it.'

Jane thrust her face into his. 'It doesn't matter if you see it,' she shouted. 'It doesn't matter if you hear it, or smell it, or have extra-fucking-sensory perception about it. All that matters is that you *do* it. So make the move, *okay*?'

'But I'm sorry for her. I want to comfort her.'

'We all know what you want to do to her,' said Jane sourly. 'You and every other man in the room apart from Rupert. But this is opera, not real life, and I *need* you over here, where the audience –

133

remember them? – can see what you're feeling. *Then Alfredo* can come and join you, leaving the stage free for *Violetta*'s next big move.'

'Oho.'

Jane raised her arms in the air. 'Oho! *Oho!* Does "oho" mean you've finally got it?'

'I got it, doll. Loud and cle-ar.'

George turned away and walked back to the piano. 'One more time then!' There was a tall young man standing there, watching them with an appreciative smile. George glowered. 'May I help you?'

'In a moment,' said the stranger. 'I wouldn't want to be responsible for confusing this move.' He grinned at George, who very reluctantly smiled back, mystified, even though he knew now that he had seen the man before.

'*Great!*' shouted Jane. 'Just *perfecto.*'

'Now?' said George to the stranger. This was the trouble with church halls. You never knew who else was going to come wandering in. They'd once been double-booked with a class of meths-drinkers and Ed had been terminally offended, when coming in to join the singers, by one of the hoboes shouting out helpfully, 'No, mate. We're over *here.*'

The man took out a card. George read it. *Paul Dumeige, 10, rue du Vallon, Lyon.* 'You are George Sinclair?'

'I am.' There was something creepy about the man. Nor did George like the scar on his nose.

134

'The owner of the company?'

'Yes. I'm afraid . . . '

Dumeige held up his hand. 'You don't remember, but we met before, at the Mansion House.'

'Oh yes!' Surely he was one of the policemen? 'You were with Commander Bright.'

'Exactly. One of my jobs is to keep your Lord Mayor safe tomorrow night. So I have come along to talk to you about this, and to enjoy your most excellent *Traviata.*' He allowed his eyes to wander over to Isabelle, and then across to Jane. One beautiful woman, and one very hot one. On the whole, he thought he preferred the latter, and from Jane's answering stare, he decided she might very well feel the same way. 'Please don't let me disturb you. I will sit here and then we can talk when you break for lunch.'

George nodded and sat down to play.

'*Georges!* Please don't start doing that again.' He'd played the wrong music.

'I liked that,' said Dumeige. 'What was it?'

'Herrmann,' said Rupert, coming over to inspect the interesting new visitor. 'The Retribution theme from . . . er . . . *Salammbô?*'

George met his enquiring gaze, and nodded. 'That's it,' he said. There was something about policemen that made him decidedly uneasy.

Chapter Twenty

It took the specialist team less than four hours to spot the significance of the call from the Black Friar Hotel through the Mansion House switchboard into Threlfall's computer line and Jerry's outward call tracing the hotel number.

'At least,' said Dumeige, excited, 'we now know where he was at six fifty-three on Monday evening.'

Bright shrugged. 'That'll be a help when we have someone to suspect. Until then, it's academic.'

'I'm sorry,' said the manager after another four hours spent searching through the police file of photographs. 'I doubt if I'd recognize him if I did see him. He was just one of hundreds.'

'You're sure he paid in cash?'

'Absolutely sure. That sort always do.'

Bright leant forward. '*That* sort?'

'Well, he had a black girl up there just before he left.'

'A tom?'

The manager shook his head. 'High class. Might

be professional, but I can tell you what she was there for.'

'Oh yes?'

'The chambermaid said she'd never seen such a mess.' He winked.

Bright stared at him. He picked up a piece of paper. 'It must have been prearranged then. This is your computer printout. He only made the one call, and that was the one we traced.'

The manager shrugged. 'Maybe. He probably had a mobile. Most businessmen do.'

'That's how he struck you? A businessman?'

The manager shook his head. 'I've told you. I can't remember anything about him. He could have been a ventriloquist for all I know.'

'You remember his paying in cash!'

'That's in the records,' said the man stubbornly.

'But I'll bet it's not in the receipts,' said Bright sourly after the manager had left.

DCI Jameson, who had sat in on the interview, nodded. 'Four sodding clients have used that room since,' he said gloomily. 'It's been blitzed by their bloody cleaners. Even so Forensic say they've found enough traces to father a regiment. But trying to sort them all out and date them will take months.'

'We still have one priceless advantage,' said Bright, leaning back in his chair.

'What's that?' asked the Chief Inspector, surprised.

'I predict that Briggs' team will be able to tell me his mobile number before long. If he was in the habit of calling in to Threlfall's computer, he'd surely have done it that way. I reckon using the hotel number was a slip-up.'

'The first he's made,' said Jameson.

'And not the last, I hope. Now, I want you to start checking on escort agencies. Start at the posh ones and work downwards. You'll have to lean on them. But I want to meet the girl.'

'Oh yes?' risked the Chief Inspector, earning a wintry frown.

'Yes. If we're right, she's the only person we know of to meet Solomon and still be alive. So if you find her, wrap her up in cotton wool, right?' The other man nodded. 'Now,' said Bright, buttoning his jacket. 'It's time for me to have another try at talking to the Lord Mayor. And this time I'm going to get at his computer backup files.'

But this apparently simple task proved less easy to complete.

'My personal computer?' Threlfall, his face a muddy grey, seemed hardly to have control over his hands at all. They busied themselves all over his desk, plying with this, snapping at that, the fingers quivering with infinitesimal movements beneath the skin.

'If we may.' Bright fixed him with a persuasive smile.

'I'm afraid that's quite impossible.' The Lord Mayor met the policeman's smile with a dismal attempt at one of his own. 'It has the most sensitive material on it, none of it relevant to poor Jerry Tomkins.'

'Nevertheless,' said the Commander, hardening his tone. 'This is a murder inquiry, and I must insist.'

'Insist?' The Lord Mayor wiped the back of his neck. 'I haven't heard that word used for a very long time.' His spirit revived a little under Bright's truculence. 'I must make a note. I've promised to call the Home Secretary before lunch. Dear Nick. He's been most kind in enquiring regularly about our predicament.'

'This is an operational matter,' said Bright, doggedly unimpressed. 'But there's no need for us to argue. We know the man who wants to kill you called in and logged on to your computer, presumably to read your files.'

'*Read my files?*' Such had been Threlfall's preoccupation with his own worries that this possible aspect of the matter had never occurred to him. 'But he can't do that! It's all coded.'

'He *could*', said Bright, 'if he knew how to gain access.'

'The *bastard!*'

Bright sat back in his chair and stared at the fat

man opposite him. Here was a man whose closest associate had just been butchered by a self-proclaimed assassin who had killed thrice before and had announced his intention of killing this same man, and imminently. Yet the first sign of any emotion he had given since the affair began was at the idea of the murderer reading his *computer files*.

'We know he accessed your computer Saturday night, and that Mr Tomkins traced the call to a local hotel.'

'Yes, that's where Jerry went.'

'I'm sorry?'

Threlfall was nodding vigorously. 'I was there. He suddenly rushed off. He did mention something about it later, but I had a major dinner, so I'm afraid I wasn't really concentrating. I never gave it another thought.'

'We think,' said Bright, frowning as he digested this extra piece of the jigsaw, 'that Solomon will have called in on other times using his mobile telephone. If so, my people may be able to trace its number through your computer files.'

Threlfall shook his head. 'It's all been erased,' he said. 'There's nothing there.'

'In that case,' said Bright stonily, 'you can have no objection to our examining—'

'In any case,' said Threlfall, interrupting, 'the Mansion House switchboard is your best bet. It's all computerized. I'm sure the numbers will be in there.

If your people search hard enough.' He smiled and rose, proffering his hand. 'Sorry not to be more help,' he said, 'but I have the City Remembrancer coming in five minutes.'

'You could have produced the Court Order, I suppose?' said Dumeige, recently returned from Fulham, when Bright joined him downstairs.

'And have ourselves kicked out of here?' said Bright. 'We have no *right* to be here, on private property. It's probably different in your country, but here we have to police by consent. My job is to stop him getting killed tomorrow night.'

'And the murderer of poor Mr Jerry Tomkins and the others?'

'Will have to wait,' said Bright. 'Make no mistake about it, Threlfall may be a crook, but he's got clout. Anyway, he may be right about the switchboard. I've got Briggs and his team on it now.'

'Good,' said Dumeige. 'Now let me tell you about the Floria Tosca Grand Opera Company.'

When he had finished, Bright rubbed his eyes. He was a tired man, having let his home problems and now his problems at work coalesce into a jumble of disquiet. He could feel a boil painfully making itself felt at the back of his neck, and now his eyes ached too.

'Well,' he said. 'And now I've got something to tell you about them.'

Dumeige looked up from his notes. 'Go on.'

'It seems that they were involved in a murder case down in Cornwall last year. Three dead, and then a suspect was shot. The police officially treated the incident as closed.' He paused.

'And unofficially . . . ' prompted Dumeige.

'That's the point, of course,' said Bright slowly. 'Unofficially they're still not entirely satisfied. It seems your friend Mister Sinclair was their chief suspect. His sister, mistress, whatever . . . '

'Mademoiselle Morny?'

'Or Mrs Winston Wheeler. She married the big coloured guy shortly afterwards. He was working without a valid visa at the time, hence the Home Office surveillance which we already knew about. Anyway, she had some sort of a motive too. They both did. The DCI in charge was happy to call it a day, but I got a call back from his assistant on the case, Detective Sergeant Skipwith. He's certain Sinclair was involved. I must say he seemed pretty persuasive.'

'Sinclair,' mused the Frenchman. 'Now what motive could he have against My Lord Mayor Threlfall?'

'Perhaps he doesn't need one,' said Bright gloomily, 'if he's a multiple murderer.'

Chapter Twenty-One

Frustrated by Threlfall's keeping to his room on Friday night, Brigadier Gooch hovered around the whole of Saturday morning, waiting his chance to inspect the Lord Mayor's Dressing Room, latterly become his mysterious computer stronghold. It was not, however, to be. Throughout the morning, after his first being woken by Frederick with his usual tray of coffee, two warm croissants and a slice of fruit cake, Reginald Threlfall had locked himself into his Dressing Room and sat in the armchair beside the empty hearth, staring at the blackened grate.

Finished. That was the unwelcome message that ground through his brain. It was over. Two weeks ago had seen his greatest triumph, borne through the streets, creaking and swaying in that massive gold carriage. And all around him were the crowds, schoolchildren, street beggars, families of the soldiers, sailors and airmen who marched in his show, all waving and cheering. A Roman triumph indeed, yet he had had no cautious slave at *his* ear, to murmur the menacing reminder that everything must end in the grave. For that hour he had thought himself immortal, he who had clawed his way to great riches and was acclaimed the hero of the City.

And now, so very soon, it was all to be taken away from him: his life by this madman, and his reputation and riches by these prowling policemen.

He had no illusions about the computers sitting silent on his and Jerry's desks. He had never really understood them, and although they seemed now to bar his access for a final gloat over his accumulated spoils, he was sure some salaried clerk in a dingy police office would easily lay bare the tawdry truth behind his wealth. For a moment he contemplated saving Solomon the trouble, and killing himself. Would that be going out in an added blaze, or would it be adding one more slice of infamy to an already overloaded plate?

He got up and stared at himself in what remained of the mirror, so gross now, his face such an ugly colour. Suddenly he smiled. He still had one trick up his sleeve. Carefully collecting his plate of uneaten breakfast, he padded back to the bedroom.

Lunch, rescheduled from the day before to entertain the Prime Warden of the Fishmongers, came and went without Threlfall putting in an appearance at all. His place was taken by a rather sheepish Aldermanic Sheriff, summoned back from a partridge shoot at his Royston seat by the increasingly harassed Private Secretary.

'But I quite understand,' said the Prime Warden for the twentieth time when faced with the Sheriff's persistent apologies. 'He's got a lot of worries, poor chap. *Please* don't say another word on the subject. It's quite all right.'

Indeed the exterior of the Mansion House now presented a dramatic picture to those who were passing, and the increasing clamour of the Press ensured that there were a great many of these. The whole of Walbrook, Poultry, Threadneedle Street, Cornhill, King William Street, and the lower part of Queen Victoria Street had been closed to traffic apart from a few vehicles with special passes driving to and from the Bank of England opposite. Police barriers were everywhere, along with the usual quota of dark blue vans. Round the corner in Upper Thames Street, in four long grey buses, their windscreens protected by wire screens, sat patient rows of uniformed men, secure in the knowledge that a police canteen had been set up in Skinners' Hall. For once the prevailing noise of this, the City's busiest junction, came not from passing traffic, but from the crackle of static on radio telephones as uniformed and plainclothes men, some openly carrying guns, moved around in preparation for the evening's performance.

Ted, the Porter, already presided over two airport

style luggage-monitors installed by the Corporation at the back of the Walbrook entrance hall after the terrorist bombs of the early Nineties. For the arrival of this audience of three hundred strangers with (presumably) a murderous fanatic among them, more monitors and a special counter-terrorist army team up from Gloucestershire were installed beside him, to his great disgust.

'No one's ever got past me,' he kept muttering to Dorothy, or Frederick, or anyone else who would listen to him.

'Don't you worry yourself, Ted!' Dorothy had squeaked back, with her high-pitched infectious giggle. 'You come upstairs when you have a free moment. Gwladys has cooked some of her cheese straws. That'll set you right.' She winked. Everyone knew that a drop of gin was what really set Ted right. He winked back.

It was four o'clock, when George and his troupe were just passing through the monitors under Captain Crookenden's cold eye, that Threlfall, casually dressed in tight cords and a bursting tweed jacket, finally emerged without speaking and just as promptly locked himself in his office downstairs.

While Jane and Ed were unpacking the costumes in the first floor Drawing Room, now designated their changing room, and George was checking over the piano as Gerard tried a few practice notes to test the acoustic, Gooch and Frederick managed to force the lock on the outer door of the Lord Mayor's Dressing Room with the help of the latter's skeleton keys.

'Ought we to be doing this?' asked the senior footman anxiously.

The Brigadier fixed him with a stern look from under his heavy brows. 'Frederick,' he said. 'I don't relish this any more than you do. But there comes a time . . . you understand, man?'

Frederick, who had also served in the Grenadiers, lowered his head. 'I know, sir.' At least no one had asked him how he came to have such a fine collection of gadgets.

'Now, you stand guard by the lift. If you hear anyone coming, knock twice and then try to head them off.' Gooch slipped into the room and shut the door behind him.

'That's all very well!' thought Frederick resentfully. 'He's the sort as always fall on their feet. What happens if the Lord Mayor comes up and catches *me* then? What'll I do to pay the mortgage?' But the Lord Mayor never emerged from his locked office downstairs, and the only people passing, Dennis with some glasses for the Boudoir cupboard and Gwladys with some clean sheets for the Lady Mayoress's bed, saw nothing strange in the Lord Mayor's footman standing guard outside his master's dressing room.

At last Gooch reappeared, looking very pale and grave.

'Everything all right, sir?' enquired Frederick, fascinated.

'No,' said the Brigadier. 'Everything is not okay. In fact,' he added in a growl, 'it's the very reverse of okay. What's that bloody awful noise?'

'I think it must be the opera star,' said Frederick gloomily.

'Opera star, my foot!' snapped Gooch. 'Sounds more like a strangled cat.' They had hurried down the service stairs which brought them to the side entrance of the Egyptian Hall. There they could see George at the piano and Gerard singing in the middle of the space left by the chairs which had been arranged round the walls leaving a hollow rectangle in the centre of the room.

A movement in the shadows behind startled them. 'Who are you?' barked Gooch.

'Oh, I'm Henry Timpson,' said the singer, emerging from behind a door. 'I'm so sorry. I was just looking round. I've read so much about this building and I've always wanted to see it. It's *wonderful.*'

'Today's the wrong day for that,' said Gooch, mollified. 'You'd better stick with the others if you don't want to get into trouble with the police.'

'Thank you,' said Henry meekly. 'I'll do that.'

Returning to the dressing room, he found Ed in a harassed state because there was no tea.

'Does it matter?' asked Bruno, his brilliantined hair shining under the chandeliers. The room had recently been repainted lime green with the mouldings picked out in pink, and the carpet looked as if some very large sea-monster had just been comprehensively sick.

'It certainly does,' said Ed, with Northern certainty. 'I can't sing without a good cup of tea.'

'We're having supper in half an hour,' called out Jane. 'There's more to worry about than your cup of tea. Have you laid out the medals?'

'I always have a cup of tea before rehearsing,' said Ed. 'What medals?'

'The *Légion d'Honneurs*, muttonhead. The ones I sent you off to Bermondsey to hire. For the party scene.'

'Oh, *those*. I thought they were buttons.'

'Anybody like a nice cup of tea?' It was Peter, fresh back from laying up the supper tables. 'Chef's brewing up in the staff canteen downstairs.'

'I could murder a cup of tea!' said Ed enthusiastically.

'Follow me,' said Peter, 'and less talk of murder, please. We're all so jumpy in this household, I can hardly hear myself think. Everyone for tea, this way. And please be careful of those new chairs. The Lord

Mayor's just had them regilded. They're his pride and joy.'

It took an increasingly frantic George nearly twenty minutes to find the missing tea-drinkers and they then rehearsed for over an hour until Peter came back to tell them that their supper was on the table. In a way, this interruption was a relief, so frantic had been the few hours they'd already had for rehearsing, and so imperfect some of their command of their parts. Most of the rehearsal indeed had been given over to the finale, since Winston still could not remember the moves he was supposed to make.

'This is going to be a hairy one,' murmured Ed to Rupert as they traipsed down the bare stone service staircase past the kitchen lift.

'When aren't they with this company?' enquired Bruno, catching them up. 'When I sing at Covent Garden, I shall insist on adequate rehearsal time.'

Ed and Rupert exchanged secret smiles. Bruno's aspirations were always as impressive as his eau-de-Cologne.

Their supper consisted of a turtle consommé, steak and kidney pudding with extra dumplings, mashed potatoes and button mushrooms and lastly a magnificent sherry trifle, the catering chef's speciality.

As a direct result of this, there was, in that

narrow room, no conversation, nothing in fact to be heard at all except a subdued and concentrated munching, and just the occasional slurp; in short, the regular and immediately recognizable sound of the Floria Tosca Grand Opera Company happily engaged in the single-minded shovelling-in of food.

It is sometimes a shock to the casual opera-goer, who imagines artistically etiolated singers starving themselves before a show because of *Art* or because of *Nerves*, to come across an opera company in action at the trough. There is a degree of fierce concentration, of sheer sweated hard labour as the feeding proceeds which jars against the aesthetic ideal. Yet this was just as George liked it. 'Give me stout singers,' he used to say, 'real trenchers, men and women such as can scent a suet pudding from fifty yards, and I'll give you an opera show to make your eyes water, and set your ears ringing for a month.' Tonight he was not so sure.

Henry, the new baritone *Marchese*, had still not been heard to give tongue. Since he was always in the chorus, it was rather hard to reproach him for this without hard evidence. When Mr Sumption, the *répétiteur*, had been playing that morning, George had sidled quietly round behind Henry's back to see if the mouthing lips were actually emitting sound. Unfortunately Maria's fit of giggling had revealed this cunning stratagem before it had borne fruit.

Nor was Rupert, as *Gastone*, doing much better.

He only had half a dozen solo lines, but had managed to mess them all up, every time. Yet both of these men were forcing down steak and kidney like there was no tomorrow.

Even Isabelle showed the strain in her eyes that the role of *Violetta* was, truthfully, beyond her. Hers was a light soubrettish soprano, ideal for *Zerlina* or *Susanna*. So she was tucking in too. The one undisputed success in casting, Gerard, the extreme-last-minute *Alfredo*, was, however, hardly eating at all. Perhaps he did suffer from nerves? George rolled his eyes and poured himself another glass of lemonade.

By the time they were back upstairs in the changing room, and could hear the bustle and drone of an arriving audience, he was convinced that this would be his last job, not least because Winston was still staring sightlessly at the last Act section of his score. There was even one heart-stopping last-minute panic. Mr Sumption had been hired for the night to turn the pages of the score for George, who had himself been unable to memorize it in time. Ten packets of Capstan and a bottle of Teacher's had been the agreed tariff, but he had still not arrived.

'I said you shouldn't have given him the cigarettes in advance,' hissed Isabelle angrily. '*Quel crapaud!*'

'He's never let me down before,' said George, trying to sound in control.

'No,' she said, 'but then you've never paid early, have you?'

'No,' he agreed. 'Isabelle, what am I to do?'

'I'll go and find Alasdair. I don't suppose he can read music, but at least he'll probably do it, if I ask him.'

Outside in the hallway, the Threlfalls stood side by side, their arms almost touching, yet light-years apart in terms of togetherness, receiving their guests, all of whom had undergone body-searches by Captain Crookenden's men (and women) from Gloucester. The Lord Mayor, his personal crisis now forgotten in his professional assumption of the role of host, positively glowed with bonhomie.

'Prosper, my dear fellow!'

'Just like our time in the School Plays, eh?' The two men, one so tall and one so broad, fairly shook with the merriment of old acquaintance.

'Fred! And Susie! You look *sensational*, my dear. He's a lucky man.'

Time passed.

'Lord Mayor,' said Gooch loudly, having stood for several minutes holding patiently on to the man's ceremonial robe in the traditional old schoolmasters' etiquette. 'I must have a word.'

Threlfall turned one frosty eye upon his Private Secretary. 'Not now, Gooch. How many more times must I tell you?'

The old soldier flushed at the public nature of

the rebuke. 'I'm sorry, Lord Mayor,' he said with dignity. 'But I have to insist.'

'*You* have to—'

'It concerns Redwood Park. Mr Bright—'

The Lord Mayor's face paled. 'I beg your pardon?'

'I'm sorry, Lord Mayor. I had to enter your Dressing Room for administrative purposes. This really is something best discussed in private. It was pure chance that I saw what I saw. Of course I haven't discussed it.'

Lady Tabley, who had been trying hard not to listen too blatantly to this hushed exchange, suddenly butted in: 'Redwood Park. The Moncktons' place? Did you buy that, Reggie? We were told it was some frightful Mafia syndicate or something.' She laughed in a suitably rustic manner.

'Excuse me.' Threlfall, who had been staring searchingly at Gooch, broke away from them, and hurried off into the crowd just as a heavy gong sounded. Peter, resplendent in his mulberry velvet, struck the Indian relic again and again with muted vigour, and its sinister reverberations echoed round the crowded rooms.

'Sounds like Armageddon,' said Colonel Lumsden, tugging at his collar. 'Or else the opera's about to begin. I'm off.'

'Aren't you going to join the merry throng?' asked Brigadier Popham who was passing, tightly contained within the City Marshal's tunic and toggles, a vision of scarlet and gold.

'Not likely. I'm taking up a defensive position . . . '

' . . . somewhere near the champagne, eh?' Both men laughed while the audience, London's richest and best-fed, edged their way cautiously through the tall double doors and into the Egyptian Hall, where George was just reminding the compliant Alasdair Rumbold of the one simple rule of turning the pages of an opera score for an accompanist: Just follow the words and turn at the *start* of the bottom line. That is to avoid straining the pianist's blood-pressure by waiting until the last possible moment when he has come to believe that the page-turner has either lost the place or, worse, nodded off.

'*Dahling!*'

'*Roger!* You old rascal!'

'*Mwaa! Mwaa!*'

A massive couple manoeuvred themselves carefully in a fruitless attempt to kiss each other's cheeks.

'And there's old *Timbo!*'

'God! I thought he was *dead.*'

'No, dahling. That's his brother.'

Grimly amused, George watched the meaty crowd filing through and then eddying out in ripples of taffeta and black serge towards the anxious little gilt chairs. He sometimes amused himself by imagining the whole audience as corpses, lolling skeletons that stared glassily through grim sockets of polished bone at the antics of his singers. Nor was there always more applause at the end of an Act than could be expected from a roomful of the sitting dead.

He turned back to Alasdair. 'It really is quite simple. Just follow the words.'

'Actually, it's all right,' said Alasdair with a smile. 'I got Grade Eight for piano myself when I was at the Royal College.'

'*You* were at the Royal College?' George stared at him. Perhaps he wasn't quite as bad as he had thought. If the man could play the piano, he couldn't be all bad.

In the middle of the long side, facing the main doors, sat the two massive gold thrones he had first seen in the hallway. Clearly these were intended for the Lord Mayor and his Lady. The latter, awash with electric blue chiffon and topped up with a diamond tiara, slightly askew, looked very uninvolved in the evening's entertainment. Twice some portly tycoon had sought to engage her attention. Both times she had continued to stare at the ceiling with glassy indifference. Perhaps she was slightly deaf?

Lady Tabley was sitting behind the Lord Mayor's empty seat, and the old bod with the walrus moustache, Pooch or Gooch, settled himself grumpily into the chair on the host's other side. Just as the room's

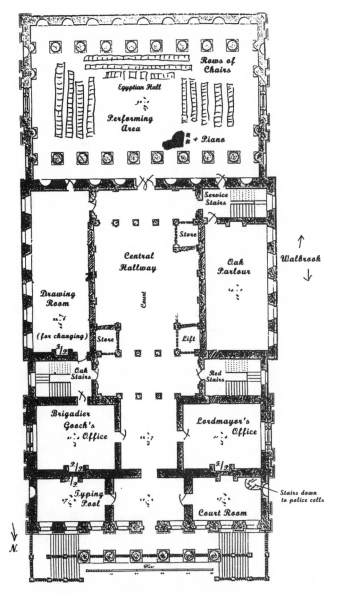

Plan of the first floor of the Mansion House

noisy conversation suddenly hushed, Frederick walked in and shouted:

'*My Lords*, *Ladies* and *Gentlemen*, pray be upstanding for the Right Honourable *The Lord Mayor*!'

Then there was a terrific bustling of dresses and a creaking of chairs, and maybe even of corsets, as three hundred people struggled to their feet.

To George's surprise, Threlfall entered *smiling*. 'That's a first,' he thought, remembering the big man's invariable bad humour.

Alasdair twitched his chair to get better placed to turn the pages, George scanned the first bars, lifted his hands and—

'Your Grace, My Lord Bishop, My Lords, Fellow Aldermen, Mr Ambassador, Ladies and Gentlemen, in short: . . . Friends!' A rumble of throaty chuckling rippled among the rows of seating and died away. The Lord Mayor had suddenly stood up again and was making a speech! George stared at Alasdair, who just shrugged. Perhaps this was how Lord Mayors always behaved at operas?

'Salman Rushdie and I . . . ' this time there was loud laughter, and then a prolonged bout of clapping. George wondered what the singers must be thinking, waiting for their musical cue to enter and now hearing what sounded like the end of the show. The Lord Mayor was well into his stride now. ' . . . this nameless assassin, who hoped to cow the civic might of our ancient Shrievalty, has more than met his match with the City of London police, than whom I think I dare boast, there are none finer!' He paused, and was rewarded by a splendid burst of 'Hear! Hear!' from many lusty throats. 'But if like Hannibal Lecter, um . . . I hope I've got that right, Dick . . . ?' he looked down at the unsmiling Brigadier Gooch beside him, and earned some more satirical chucklings at the thought of the Brigadier's supposed expertise in this field, ' . . . he chose me as victim for his next meal, then indeed he can safely exercise the Judgement of Solomon and still be assured of a hearty feast!

'But, seriously, my dear friends. My wife and I bid you a most cordial and heartfelt welcome to our humble home. Tonight's performance by the . . . er . . . Florence Tosca Company . . . of whom you will all have heard, I know, is being undertaken to raise money for our brave Lifeboatmen, a fund than which there is none closer to my heart. As a sailor,' he was in danger of getting carried away and corrected himself hastily, 'or at least as one who would always have liked to be a sailor, I know what sacrifices and dangers these doughty seafarers face. Your being here tonight has already ensured a clear profit of . . . ' He turned towards Lady Tabley who mouthed at him. 'Yes. Of seventeen thousand pounds, with more to come from the raffle after supper. In this context I particularly want to thank the great City institution of Schumann and Gold-water, I see my dear friends Mr and Mrs Fred Tevis are here with us this evening, for their most generous sponsorship. But enough from me! Let the music commence, and if Solomon is in our midst,' there was a collective intake of breath, 'let us hope that he likes opera!'

He sat down to prolonged applause, which he acknowledged by a half-rise from his chair describing a broad semicircle with his triumphant smile. *Now don't fucking fall asleep,* he muttered out of the corner of his mouth while miming a loving smile at his wife.

She smiled back, and murmured, *Sod you too.*

He waved a lordly hand at George, the lights suddenly dimmed and George struck the opening chords with unusual violence. *La Traviata* had begun.

Chapter Twenty-Two

As it turned out, all Winston's careful rehearsing of the last Act proved unnecessary. For it was just as *Flora's* Act 2 party reached its climactic moment that disaster struck.

Alfredo, singing like a dream, had confronted *Violetta*, her long blonde wig still securely framing the beautiful pathetic face of a doomed courtesan thanks to Jane's hat pin. Calling back the other party-goers, in this case Maria, Jane, Bruno and Rupert, (Henry having finally given up the unequal struggle and stayed slumped in his changing room chair), Gerard pulled out the money he'd just 'won' from Bruno and raised it to strike an anguished-looking Isabelle when suddenly all the lights went out.

There was a shout and then, shockingly, the flash and roar of a gun going off.

Alasdair, who had just been preparing to turn the page for George, leapt up, overturning his chair in his alarm. There was screaming everywhere. George saw another flash and then felt rather than heard someone blundering past the piano. There was a long stunned silence, and then at last a policeman on the balcony above them produced a flashlight and after another few moments of bedlam, light was restored.

When the crowd cleared, George could see the angry stout man with the big white moustache still sitting rigidly upright in his chair next to the Lord Mayor's throne, with a ragged black hole where his left eye had been.

But of the Lord Mayor, there was no trace at all.

Chapter Twenty-Three

'*Where is the Lord Mayor?*'

How many times had that question been asked? Frantic security guards, stumbling guests, confused singers, a white-faced Commander Bright: all of them repeated the same words, over and over, as they herded blindly through the stifling throng, with the air thick with the stink of fear.

George, impatient of the chaos, had slipped up the big wooden side staircase to find somewhere peaceful to sit, and think. Turning left through a pedimented doorway, he found himself in a wide dark rectangular passage, with walls painted a muted blue behind a mass of ornamental carving and furnished with two immense blue velvet sofas.

On one of these sat Charlotte Threlfall, scarlet in the face, fanning herself with one of the opera programmes.

'Bloody hell!' she muttered, and looking up, waved at him. 'Come and sit down here, *maestro*!'

George did as he was told. There was a long

silence during which his hostess heaved a number of heavy sighs. At last, feeling pressured, he said, 'Quite a drama.'

She leant forward and then turned her body dramatically towards him. 'Quite a *fucking* drama, you think? You think it's quite a *fucking* drama?' He nodded helplessly, unable to meet her burning gaze. 'Let me tell *you* something . . . ' she prodded his knee with one forceful, though not entirely accurate, finger, ' . . . it's the best bloody day of my life.'

'You like opera?'

'*Opera!*' She let out a screech of laughter. '*Hate* the buggers!'

'But . . . ?'

'My *husband*, my dear man. Somebody's got rid of the bastard. If there's any justice in this fucking world, they'll chop him up for bloody *catfood!*' Her voice had risen to a highly unmusical shriek. Colonel Lumsden sat watching this scene on Video Screen 6, now that the system had been restored to life after being blacked out by the power failure. The basement command station echoed with her words, and he couldn't help smiling at the volatile expressions on George's face.

'Where's that?' Paul Dumeige had suddenly joined him.

'*There* you are!' said the Colonel, much relieved. 'We've got real trouble. Poor old Gooch is dead, shot, and the Lord Mayor's disappeared.'

'I know that,' said Dumeige impatiently, peering over his shoulder, 'but that video . . . ?'

'The Blue Corridor. Just outside the Ballroom.'

'Second floor?'

'Got it.'

'It's a dreadful picture. If only they'd put in an emergency supply, we'd have all the answers on tape. Who's with Madame Threlfall?'

'Opera chap. I can't remember his name. He runs the show.'

'What's he saying?'

The Colonel turned up the volume.

'Weren't . . . you . . . sitting . . . next . . . to . . . him?' George was enunciating slowly and clearly, praying she wasn't going to prod him again.

'Next to him? I'm always effing next to him.' She rolled her eyes. 'This house gives me the creeps. Sometimes I feel he's spying on me through the walls. Biggest mistake of my fucking life!' She waggled her head at him, and suddenly wiped her mouth with the back of her hand in a strange unpleasant gesture.

George stared. 'What was?'

'Was what?' She giggled and wagged her finger at him.

'The biggest mistake?'

This time she laughed out loud. '*Marrying* the bastard. Still,' she waggled her head again, 'let's look on the bright side as Mr Wotsisname, the Steward

165

or whatever, always says . . . ' She seemed to have momentarily lost her drift. Her eyes faded from their fierce intensity and she started scratching her knee. George, suddenly depressed, waited. '*Ed-wards!*' she yodelled. 'That's his name, the Steward. As Mr *Edwards* says, let's look on the bright side and hope the bastard's *dead meat!*'

Downstairs, Colonel Lumsden turned the volume back down. 'Poor woman.'

Paul Dumeige shrugged. 'When a woman drinks . . . I might be more inclined to feel sorry for the husband.'

'Not in this case,' said the Colonel firmly, and switched to Channel 5, the one showing a bird's-eye view of the empty Ballroom. 'I remember her as a girl. A fine woman on a horse. Threlfall wrecked her life, among others.'

Before their eyes, Dennis the youngest footman slipped through a door, with one of the opera guests holding his hand. After a brief guilty look round at the apparently empty Ballroom, he began to kiss her.

Lumsden chuckled. 'Nice to know some things never change,' he said and switched channels again, this time to Channel 3, which covered the entrance lobby to the Egyptian Hall. There the crowd was almost rioting, as people fought their way first one way, then the other, with no discernible purpose other than some innate urge to keep moving. They could make out Bright, surrounded by men in uniform. To his left Lord Tabley towered above a gaggle of anxious women, and, in another corner, Isabelle, in a negligée, was receiving the homage of a number of star-struck fans.

'Your men are still searching?' It was Lumsden who put the question, though either could have done so, since there were as many men under Lumsden's private control in the great building as there were policemen.

Dumeige nodded, and asked again, 'He can't have got out?'

Lumsden shook his head. 'Every door was barred, and I've checked with the men in the street too. Not a cat!'

'What about the fire-escapes?'

'All checked.'

'The roof?'

'Completely clear.'

'The tube exit?'

Lumsden stared. 'I'm sorry?'

Dumeige smiled. 'Oh, Colonel, I do know about your precious secret.'

Lumsden went rather red in the face. 'My secret?'

'The metal door? Into the Bank underground? A14? The counter-terrorist command centre?' The Frenchman pretended to search deep in his memory. 'There are two keys, aren't there? Yours and the City Commander's, yes?'

The Colonel nodded angrily. 'You shouldn't know all this,' he blurted.

Dumeige smiled. 'The fight against crime is global,' he said, almost like a child reciting a mnemonic. 'If we do not pool our resources, the gangsters will win.' The Colonel just continued to glare at his feet. 'Do not be angry, Colonel. Much of your defences are on the Interpol computer. So are ours, and the Americans. It is the key to global success against crime.'

'I *hate* computers,' growled the older man. 'Bloody untrustworthy and not secure. Not secure at all!'

Dumeige nodded in sympathy. 'There you are in the right! But look!'

The scanner had continued to change channels automatically, and now had focused on two men, clearly arguing.

'Where is that?' Lumsden turned up the volume, while also pressing the button to zoom in closer on the couple.

'I'm going home, and now!' It was one of the opera singers, the bulky black baritone named Winston, and he was standing nose to nose with Ted, the Porter at the main Walbrook entrance.

'I'm very sorry, sir!' Ted's voice was sharpened

with anger, and just a little slurred. 'No one is leaving this building. Them's the orders.'

'You can open the door,' said Winston calmly, 'or I can tear it off its fucking hinges.' He grinned into the other man's flushed face. 'Your choice, *smiler.*'

Ted seemed to swell. 'There's no call for that sort of talk, *sir . . .* '

Colonel Lumsden depressed another button, holding it down. 'Oh, Ted?' His voice boomed over the loudspeaker by the desk.

Both men turned, startled. 'Yes, sir?' said the Porter.

'Ask the gentleman from the opera to return to the dressing room, please.'

Winston saw the video camera and advanced towards it, until his contorted face filled the screen. 'Listen, *Sir,* I came here to sing. I'm paid till ten thirty and it's after eleven. I'm sorry some arsehole blew a lump out of Mister Pastry, but I've got another job to go to, and I'm not staying here, not even for your *charming* friend down here. Get it?'

'Winston Wheeler,' murmured the Colonel's assistant who had come in during this exchange and had smartly tapped some keys on another computer. 'Born Trinidad 21 May 1971, considered for deportation for working while on student visa last year. Married Isabelle Morny, she's in the troupe too, 14 December 1995. Home Office maintaining a

Section 17 monitoring surveillance. They think they've got a strong case for deportation.'

'Hello, Mr Wheeler,' said Dumeige, cutting in urbanely over the loudspeaker. 'How're you doing down there?'

'Fucking awful!' But the giant sounded mollified by the personal tone.

'I've got to advise you against opening the outer door.'

'Oh yeah?'

'Mmm. There's a streetful of policemen out there, and they're going to enjoy beating the shit out of you if they think you're trying to escape.'

'No kidding?'

'No kidding. The Colonel's right. You would do better to go back to the dressing room and wait there with your wife.' Dumeige allowed a little friendly chuckle into his voice, and got an answering wink from the big man directed at the video camera. His nose must have been almost touching the lens.

'And who are you then, pal?' he called out.

'Paul Dumeige,' came the answer over the loud-speaker. '*Sous-Commandant*. At your service.'

'Winston Wheeler, *greatest of baritones*, at yours,' came the amiable retort, and they watched the big singer amble peaceably out of shot, back towards the dressing room upstairs.

*

George meanwhile, having escaped the conversation of Charlotte Threlfall by the simple means of staying firmly on the sofa when she staggered to her feet and teetered off through the door into the Ballroom in search of a lavatory, sat staring at the ceiling.

For some minutes now George's mind had been concentrating on a new, and awful, presentiment. Might not the police still suspect him of being involved in the murders down in Cornwall? Not only had the real murderer tried to kill Isabelle in front of three witnesses, but ample corroborative evidence had subsequently been uncovered by Chief Inspector Dyle, the local CID man in charge. But the sergeant, DS Skipwith or whatever his name was, had made it pretty clear that George's proper place was behind bars. On a permanent basis. 'I'd like to slit your greasy throat,' growled George aloud, startling the Steward, old Mr Edwards, who was passing through from the Boudoir with a tray of used glasses.

'I beg your pardon, sir,' he said politely, regarding George's presence on the velvet sofa with just a touch of implied rebuke. 'I didn't see you there.' Then, seeing George's troubled expression, he added, in a kindlier tone, 'Can I get you a drink, sir?'

George shook his head. 'No, thank you,' he said. 'All I want is to get out of here without being arrested for kidnapping the Lord Mayor! Where on earth could he have got to?'

The tall old man smiled with his eyes. 'I've

worked in this house for nearly sixty years,' he said. 'It's a fine building. But if the Nazis,' he pronounced the word *narzzies*, 'had hit us, instead of messing about with all those beautiful churches, I reckon some people'd have had a shock.' George stared at him, totally lost. 'I mean,' said the Steward, unbending completely, 'it's all happened before.'

'*Happened before?*' George could hardly believe his ears. Someone else had shot the Lord Mayor's Private Secretary in full view of three hundred people and then made off with the great man himself?

'I mean,' said Mr Edwards gravely, 'another Lord Mayor vanished here. They never found him either.' He put his tray down on a table with a grateful sigh.

'It's a bit soon to say that,' protested George. 'Perhaps he's hiding in a cupboard. I can't say I'd blame him with this Solomon man on the loose.'

Mr Edwards shook his head. 'They never found the other one,' he said, almost with pride. 'Though they looked for ever so long.'

'When was this?' asked George, intrigued.

'1745,' said the old man portentously.

'*1745?*'

The old man nodded. 'After the Jacobite Rebellion. The then Lord Mayor was thought to have lent them millions. But when the militia came for him, he just got up from the table, as cool as you please, left the room, *and they never saw him again.*'

'I didn't realize the house was as old as that,' said George looking round. It all looked pretty new to him, especially with all the fresh paint and the grey video camera with its bloodshot winking eye.

'Only just,' was the wheezing reply. 'They started building in 1739, and they were still messing about with the Egyptian Hall in 1753, but the main building was occupied in 1744. That Lord Mayor, Sir Wilbraham Something . . . um . . . Smith his name was, I believe, had quite a hand in the designing of it. But when you've been in a job as long as I have,' he winked very solemnly, 'you know when to keep *schtumm*. But it's been nice, seeing old friends tonight.' He looked at his watch and coughed hoarsely. 'I must get back down to the Parlour.' He picked up the tray and hurried out, a bent but highly impressive figure. George watched him leave, and shook his head. It was all a different world.

The Ballroom door opened a crack and one of the footmen peeped out at him. George pretended to be tying his shoe-lace.

'Sir?'

He looked up, acting surprise. 'Hello?'

'Has Mr Edwards gone?'

'He went down to the Parlour, or so he said.'

The young man tiptoed out, holding a young woman by the hand. Her dress was very dishevelled and some make-up had found its way on to the man's dress collar. 'Would you mind just checking the stair-case for me?'

George nodded and walked over to the farther door. He looked out. 'All clear,' he said. 'Your . . . er . . . zip . . . '

The young man looked down and blushed a deep red. 'Thanks.' The couple hurried out. As soon as they were out of sight, he heard suppressed giggling, and smiled to himself. It wasn't so long ago that Isabelle and he . . . his smile died away. Where was she now? With that bloody stuck-up Sir Alasdair Rumfuckingbold, no doubt! Lapping up the praise, and much else besides. Furious, he kicked the heavy pillar beside the doorway.

'Mr Sinclair?'

It was the French policeman, Dumeige, coming through from the service staircase.

'Yes?'

'Would you join us in Brigadier Gooch's office?'

'Now?'

'Now.' His tone did not encourage delay, so George, his mind still churning, followed him back down the oak stairs.

'Mister Sinclair!' Bright was all bonhomie. 'Thank you *so* much.'

'My pleasure,' said George sourly.

'I've been hearing about your earlier brush with murder.' George kept his face perfectly still. 'Chief

Inspector Dyle of Truro CID speaks most highly of you.'

'That's nice to hear.'

Bright grinned. 'DS Skipwith is less forthcoming.'

'I can imagine!'

'It seems you had a lucky escape.'

'My sister had a lucky escape,' said George. 'She was damn nearly killed. It was only thanks to a friend of mine she didn't end on a slab herself.'

'Your *sister*,' said Bright, reading his notes. 'Mrs Wheeler. That's right, isn't it, though it seems she spends much of her *time* with you?'

'How can I help you?' said George, suddenly impatient.

'Put yourself in our shoes,' said Dumeige. 'That is an expression, isn't it?' The others nodded. 'Here we have one innocent old man shot in front of us. Another, the First Gentleman of the City of London, is apparently abducted in his own house, and here, in our midst, is a man apparently still a suspect in a murder case on the occasion of another opera. What are we to think?'

George fairly shook with frustration. 'The other case was open and shut. As clear as—'

'A *pikestaff*?' enquired Dumeige, with slight diffidence.

'If you must. The Lord Mayor has been publicly threatened by this madman. Hasn't he killed people in Germany and New York?' George could hear his voice quivering. 'I haven't left London for *months.* That's easily checked.'

Bright spread his hands on the dead man's desk. 'Perhaps what you say is true,' he conceded. 'But it was during *your* opera show that this happened. Can you for example tell me where you were at six fifty-three this Monday evening?'

George felt his face tingling. 'You are serious, aren't you?' he said, in a voice of wonder. He wrinkled his forehead. Monday? He could hardly remember where he'd been the night before! Six fifty-three, for God's sake.

'*Yes!*'

'I'm sorry?' Bright looked up from making notes.

'I can tell you where I was,' said George triumphantly. 'I was just getting out of my bath, at Number Thirty-Seven, Bonsor Street, Hammersmith.'

'Any witnesses?'

'Certainly. Isabelle was with me, and she went downstairs to join Sir Alasdair, who was taking her to the opera, so they can both confirm it. I, at least, have an alibi.'

'But the shot came from where? You and Sir Alasdair were just the two of you at the keyboard, weren't you?'

George nodded. 'The bang could have been from anywhere. Then I felt the bloody bullet go past us. It must have been fired from somewhere near the service doorway. Anyway I wasn't alone. Sir Alasdair was with me. He can tell you I wasn't firing a gun at anyone. Nor was he. We had enough to do being the bloody orchestra.'

'What we haven't told you,' said Dumeige, leaning over him, 'is that there were *two* bullets. The explosion you heard was the first. The one you felt must have been the second.'

'*Two* bullets?'

Bright nodded. 'One went through Brigadier Gooch's eye, while the other . . . '

' . . . hit the Lord Mayor's chair,' said Dumeige, suppressing a high-pitched giggle. 'It's a miracle it didn't kill him.'

'Or whoever was sitting behind him!' said George, puzzled.

Bright nodded. 'Yes. But whoever fired that second bullet was using soft-nosed ammunition. It would have made a right mess of the Lord Mayor the way it was aimed. But for some reason . . . ' he wrinkled his brow.

' . . . he must have moved,' said Dumeige. 'Though why?'

'If we can figure that out,' said Bright, 'we might know where he is now. Anyway, the bullet just flattened itself against the wooden frame. A normal one would have gone right through and probably killed Lady Tabley.'

'I didn't see her husband,' said George.

Bright sniffed. 'He told me he hated opera. He was sitting it out in the Lord Mayor's Boudoir upstairs, reading the evening paper.'

'Oh?' George frowned. 'But I still don't understand. I only heard one shot.'

Bright rubbed his eyes. 'Probably using a silencer.'

'*Yes!*' breathed George.

'What?' said the other two men in unison.

'There *was* a second tiny flash. Later.'

Dumeige leant over him. 'Now *think hard*,' he said excitedly. 'This is important. Where did the second flash come from?'

George closed his eyes. After a pause he shook his head. 'I'm sorry,' he said. 'A flash is a flash. It could have come from anywhere.'

Bright blew out his cheeks. 'This is a bloody nightmare,' he said, and slammed his hand down on the desk.

A uniformed officer came slowly in, a look of despair on his face. 'We've found another body,' he said.

Chapter Twenty-Four

At the top of the oak staircase on the second floor
was a small lobby, leading eventually either left to
the Boudoir or straight through to the Blue Corridor,
where George had been sitting with Mrs Threlfall
only a short time before. It was made all the more
impressive, as lobbies go, by a heavy stone fireplace.
There, sprawled incontinently across the top step of
the stairs, lay the crumpled figure of a woman. DCI
Jameson was kneeling beside her, and a white-faced
Frederick, the Lord Mayor's footman, was leaning
uselessly against the further doorway.

'Who is it?'

Jameson looked up to Frederick, who hurriedly
turned away, one hand clawing at a handkerchief.
'It's one of the maids,' he said, 'as far as I can make
out.' He gestured at the heaving figure of Frederick.
'Dorothy . . . Dorothea?'

'Dorothy.' Dennis, the youngest footman, had
come through the doorway. He seemed much more
in control of himself. 'What's happened?'

'She's been bloody shot,' muttered Frederick. 'Right in the throat, poor cow.'

Jameson pulled off his jacket and laid it gently over her. She had never seemed large in life. In death she appeared no bigger than a child. 'Same calibre as the Brigadier, I'd say. .38 or thereabouts. Definitely not soft-nosed.'

Bright nodded. 'But why *two* guns?'

'Look!' It was Dumeige who grabbed his arm and pointed. There, in the upper corner of the space, was one of their video cameras, winking prettily. 'We've got the whole thing on tape. At least we weren't blacked out this time.' He turned and ran lightly down the stairs.

'*No!*' A woman's scream, and the door behind Dennis was thrown open. '*No! Don't say it's true!*' Gwladys, her craggy face all awry and her lips forced back by her terrible cry, flung herself on the little bundle on the floor, twisting her shoulder away from Jameson's half-hearted efforts to restrain her. 'Not Dorothy! Not my little lovely!' She turned a pitiful face towards Frederick, tears running from her eyes and nose, 'Oh Fred! They've taken her from me. They've . . . there was no need . . . she'd never hurt no one . . . ' She turned back, and collapsed sobbing quietly on the body of her friend. 'They *needn't* . . . '

Bright, feeling tears at the back of his own eyes, trudged heavily down the stairs. However many deaths he had seen, the loss felt by the bereaved never failed to move him. In a way, it uplifted him. He, who was so used to the cruel indifference of those who killed and wounded others, was moved but also reassured by signs of the genuine care of one human being for another.

When he reached the control room, Dumeige was already rerunning the tapes. It took some time to isolate the right camera, which was angled in such a way as to cover the door and the landing, but not the staircase.

At last they were able to watch, transfixed, as first Peter came into shot, carrying a tray. He paused, looked around, and then balancing the tray on one steady hand, he opened the door and went through. 'There's a long gap here, you can hear some of the opera in the distance, that's all,' said Dumeige, fast-forwarding the tape. Then Dorothy, the little old maid came through the doorway from the opposite direction, stared at the empty space, took a step towards the fireplace, half-turned and said something inaudible. Immediately there was the muffled, but unmistakable, sound of a shot and she put out one hand before slowly collapsing across the top step of the stairs. Throughout this whole distasteful show, the lobby had been entirely empty. And although they kept the tape running for another eighteen minutes until Frederick came through the door with a bottle and found her, there was no sight of her murderer, not even the shadow of his progress.

'What do you make of that?' said Bright after a long, long silence.

'I suppose,' said Dumeige doubtfully, 'it must have come from behind her.'

'Well, it didn't,' snapped Jameson, unusually upset by what he had just watched. 'She was shot square in the throat. The bullet's still lodged in the vertebrae. Dr Rivett's up there now.'

'He was hiding in the fireplace,' said Bright. 'That's the only way.'

'He must be damn small then,' said Jameson. 'Even I would have difficulty getting in there. Let alone firing a shot.'

'Get Forensic on to it. He must have gone back downstairs again. What's immediately below?'

'The Drawing Room. Where the opera singers are changing.'

'I see,' said Bright in a dry tone. 'Have the guests all gone?'

DS Reynolds, who had been in charge of the screening, had come back into the room. 'Yes, sir. They'll all be over at Cannon Street now. It'll be a long night! I've just kept the opera singers, the catering staff and Lady Threlfall's friends as instructed.'

Bright nodded. Then, without another word, he, Dumeige and Jameson returned upstairs via the oak staircase to the central hall, last seen in chaos, now hushed and as calm as could be expected, with armed police officers and half a dozen dogs combing the rooms, but without knowing for what they searched.

'What I don't understand,' he sighed, thrusting his hands into his pockets, and turning his head slowly from side to side, 'is how this man is moving around without our spotting him.'

Dumeige was blowing his nose. 'Or how he managed to get two guns into the building through all your precautions! Surely,' he went on, 'we have to consider a radical alternative. We have been assuming that Solomon would have to try to penetrate our defences.'

'Yes.'

'But what, *Commandeur*, if he was able to move among us with complete impunity?'

'You mean disguised again?' Bright shook his head. 'Look around you. There are no false beards in this building.'

Nor looking around them at the hushed lobby did that seem an unreasonable assertion. There was Isabelle on a sofa with George and Alasdair, who had just come back from the cloakroom, old Mr Edwards was shuffling back towards the service door with Peter and Dennis in ceremonial attendance upon him. Lord Tabley, towering over Bruno and the chubby but comparatively diminutive Colonel

Lumsden, was explaining some complicated theory of ballistics to them, while through the open doorway, they could see the other singers passing and repassing, impatient to be released.

All those bare revealing faces, naked as born, yet somewhat altered, progressively smudged by the passing of time. Their very innocence lent an added significance to the one feature available: 'I don't suppose', added Bright on spotting it, 'you want me to pull the Colonel's moustache to see if it's real.'

But Dumeige was not diverted. 'I mean,' he persisted, *what if Solomon were one of us?*'

Bright stared at him. 'You mean, here. In this room?'

'Yes,' said Dumeige. 'Mr Sinclair. Lord Tabley. Sir Rumbold. Or even one of these soft-footed servants.' Frederick was bearing down on them with a last tray of sausage rolls. Suddenly, seen with Dumeige's eyes, he had a new, menacing air about him. He offered his tray, but Bright waved him away nervously. 'I think you ask them all to account for their movements on Monday night, starting with Lord Tabley. To me, he has quite the air of Sir Hopkirk.'

'I didn't know you'd ever met him,' said Bright vaguely, 'but I will think about it.' He glowered over at where Isabelle was, rather unsuitably, laughing at something George had said.

'They none of them know about the maid,' said

Dumeige, as if in mitigation of their carefree emotions. 'This must seem very strange to them.'

'Not in this company's case,' said Bright in an acid tone. 'They are not unused to bloody murder.'

The two policemen walked on to Gooch's office where a second, more elaborate, incident room was being set up by a number of civilians wearing photo-tags. Removals men were passing backwards and forwards, with all the usual impedimenta, and a British Telecom engineer was arguing about the routing of new cables with Brigadier Popham.

Seeing them go, George stood up. 'I don't like this,' he said. 'Why haven't they let us go with all the others?'

'Perhaps they know your reputation?' said Isabelle with a sly smile.

'What reputation?' Alasdair was intrigued.

'It's nothing,' said George, suddenly angry. 'It's just that—'

'Thank God I've found you,' gasped Jane running over to them. 'It's Gerard.'

'Who?'

'Your *Alfredo*, you idiot. The new man. He's got a gun hidden in his jacket.'

'You can't be serious.'

'Oh no!' hissed Jane furiously. 'Likely I'd come and make that up just to liven up a dull evening. Listen, *birdbrain*. Either help me, or I'm going to stand here and *scream* until somebody comes.'

George placed a hasty hand over her opening mouth. 'Okay, okay. I'll come and see. You sure it was a gun?'

'Well, it had a handle and a trigger, but maybe you're right. Maybe he was just getting overexcited at the sight of Maria's D-cup.'

'Which pocket?' They were hurrying back towards the changing room.

'Inside left of his jacket. It might be in a holster. I only saw it for a moment when he came in after the shooting. You're going to have the mother of all dry-cleaning bills too. He smells like a wombat.'

'Where is he now?'

'In here with the rest. He's down by the far window, watching the crowd outside in the street. He couldn't leave because they put policemen on all three doors after Winston tried to march off. What are we going to do?'

'Grab it,' said George tersely.

'Shouldn't we tell the police?'

'And have them bugger it up like that poor sod in the performance? Winston and Ed will sort him out.'

'Oh thanks. I'm glad I came for you. Now I can be a widow too.'

'Look,' said George, stopping and grasping her upper arm. 'He won't suspect us. But imagine what'll happen if half a dozen plods charge into the room. We'll all be dead by the time they've worked out which one he is.' They walked into the room. 'And anyway,' he continued, 'I'd like to try another rehearsal next week. There are one or two other people who just might employ us now we've got a production on the *tapis*. Uh, Winston?'

'Yup?'

'A word about your cadenza, please? And Ed?'

The three men went into a momentary huddle and then split, with George walking straight over towards Gerard, while Ed and Winston sidled round via the ironing board to take him in the rear.

'Um . . . Gerard.'

The man looked up. Now that George knew about the gun, he realized he had never felt entirely easy with the tenor. For one thing, he was too normal, too buttoned-up, without the usual tenor's preoccupation with his vocal chords. 'You sang really well tonight.'

'Thank you, George.' The tenor smiled with relaxed satisfaction. 'I enjoyed it very much. Quite a change.'

'I hope we can do some more work together . . . ' Ed grabbed the man's neck from behind, while Winston swept his legs from under him and the three of them went down in a flurry of grunts and flailing arms.

But it did not go as it should have gone, three against one. Gerard headbutted Winston so hard the big baritone jack-knifed backwards with an anguished cry, and immediately Gerard and Ed were thrashing around while George hovered helplessly.

'Hit the bastard!' cried Ed, trying to gouge an eye. George grabbed Gerard's hair which slipped greasily through his fingers while Jane aimed a blow at him with a wine bottle but missed, shattering it against Ed's head instead.

'You fools,' croaked Gerard, who was now holding George by the throat, 'I'm a . . . '

Isabelle, still top-heavy with her wig, ran at him and kneed him in the crotch with a swingeing upwards thrust, and then as the anguished man fell gasping forward, George grabbed up one of the gilded chairs and brought it smashing down on his shoulders, breaking its legs in the process. Immediately he felt other hands pulling at him and wrenched himself free.

'Hello,' said a familiar voice from the doorway. 'Up to your usual tricks, Mr Sinclair? Striking a police officer in the course of his duty *and* now resisting arrest. Book him!'

'Why, Sergeant Skipwith!' panted George from the floor where he had fallen. 'This is an unexpected pleasure.'

Three uniformed men hustled him out of the room.

Chapter Twenty-Five

The first-floor room in the north-west corner of the Mansion House has long functioned as a Magistrate's Court, the only one still situated in a private house.

Despite temporary suspension in the Eighties, this Court now deals again with minor infractions of the law within the Square Mile of the historic City, and beneath it, reached from the dock by a spiral stone staircase, and from the ground floor via the silver vaults, are two fully equipped police cells, complete with individual toilets.

It was here, an hour later, that Isabelle and Alasdair Rumbold came with news that Commander Bright had reluctantly ordered George's release.

'It was Prosper,' said Alasdair. 'He soon sorted it out. These policemen are *impossible* sometimes.' Some sort of change had overtaken him. He seemed suddenly older, and less vital, as if the shock of the night's events had, slowly, begun to affect him.

George smiled at them wearily. It was affecting him too. 'Actually, it was rather peaceful down here,' he said. 'After Sergeant Skipwith went away. Our Gerard is better known hereabouts as Detective Chief Inspector Perry Piper of Special Branch. Would you have guessed that he leads the Metropolitan Police Choir?'

Isabelle stared, and shook her head. 'No,' she said. 'I wouldn't have.'

'Well, he does. What's more he's asked me to play at their next concert at the Old Bailey. Though after your attentions, he thinks he may be singing treble again.'

'*Bon.*'

George sighed. 'It's quiet down here.'

'And safe,' sneered Isabelle, with feeling. 'But I can remember what it was like in Cornwall even if you can't. Your friend upstairs can't wait to lock you up again. We've got to solve this one ourselves before they decide to put you back down here and throw away the key.'

George stared at them. 'How can we catch this maniac? We don't even know what he looks like!'

'We did it last time,' said Isabelle, shaking him. 'Come *on, Georges*! Wake yourself up. Think!'

'Think about what?'

'Well,' she said. 'Let's work it out.'

'*I think I might be able to help.*'

'What?'

Standing behind them was Henry, the silent baritone, blinking shyly. 'I followed you down.'

'You did?' Isabelle stared at him. She'd never really looked at him before. Behind that stooped and self-effacing mien, she saw, for the first time, a face of considerable strength and unexpected self-assurance.

'Yes,' he said, with a slight smile. 'When not singing, I study architectural history and I've been preparing an article on Catholic priest's holes for *The Tablet*. This building is one of great unsolved mysteries, which is why I was so interested in taking on the work here.'

'And?' She could see George making winding motions with his arm. They really hadn't time for the cubby-holes of history with a maniac on the loose.

'There's no reason why you should know this,' he went on, unperturbed. 'But a famous figure in Jacobite mythology,' she had to bite her lip to stop herself from yelling at him, 'was Lord Mayor of London in 1745. The Hanoverians tried to arrest him here, but he *disappeared.*'

'That's true,' broke in George. 'The old Steward was telling me about this upstairs.'

'There was a famous Welsh family called Owen.'

'So famous even I've never heard of them,' drawled Alasdair.

Henry smiled diffidently. 'That's why I'm studying them for my thesis. You see it was a bit like in Northern Ireland, or in Bosnia, in those days.

Both sides did terrible things to each other. So the Roman Catholics took to building priest's holes all over their houses, in case the Protestant agents ever came to arrest them.'

'I thought it was the Catholics who burnt people,' said Alasdair sourly, ignoring Isabelle's outraged glare.

'So they did,' said Henry. 'But James I used to delight in torturing priests himself. It was just a game to him, pulling bits off those poor men in the Tower after dinner.'

'Please,' said George. 'How is this relevant?'

'Sir Wilbraham Smith was a secret Catholic. He was one of the three Aldermen placed in charge of building the Mansion House. One theory is that he already knew about Prince Charles Edward's plans, and thought to protect himself by building a priest's hole, or more probably several priest's holes, in this building.'

'Without the architect knowing?' asked Alasdair incredulously.

'Yes! That's the point about the Owen family. They would get work on the site, ordinary work, joiners, whatever. Then, when the other men had knocked off, the Owens would be secretly digging and constructing inner chambers. Nicholas Owen, he was known as *Little John*, was the first. He built priest's holes all over the country, double panelling, false flues, trapdoors, the works. They say Hindlip

Hall in Worcestershire had more holes than a Gruyère cheese. That's where they caught him eventually.'

'Who did?'

'Lord Salisbury's men. They starved him out after seven days. He was tortured to death in the Tower of London on 2 March 1606.'

'You do know your homework,' said Alasdair, with a hint of weariness.

'Which is more than he can say of *Traviata*,' murmured George to Isabelle.

'What?'

'What I want to know,' said Isabelle stepping in tactfully, 'is what a false flue is?'

'That's easy,' said Henry, his eyes gleaming. 'You have two flues. One is for the smoke, but the other, with an entrance through false bricks sooted up to conceal its existence, is for a fugitive.'

Alasdair was still frowning. 'You said Owen was executed in 1606. This building is surely eighteenth-century.'

'Begun in 1738,' stated George.

The others stared at him.

'How on *earth* did you know that?' asked Henry, with unflattering amazement.

George shrugged. 'One knows these things.'

'Well, you're right,' said Henry, still staring at him. 'Exactly right. But the point about the Owens is they were a dynasty, like the Adam family or the Wyatts. For as long as Roman Catholics were persecuted, there were Owens from Pontypool to dig them refuges. They were a right bunch of badgers!'

'And you think *an* Owen, one of the family, worked here, secretly, in this building?' Isabelle's eyes were shining too. 'How *romantic*!'

'So all we need to do now,' said George, 'is find our way in, and with luck we'll find one desperate Lord Mayor in fear of his life, and a raging lunatic with at least two handguns! In the dark too! I think I'm going back to *thés dansants* in Seaford!'

Isabelle was staring at the floor, her head cocked on one side. 'What,' she said, and paused. 'What if this was something quite different?'

'You mean you don't think there's some anonymous lunatic loose in those corridors?' asked Alasdair, who had resumed his air of fatigue.

'I mean,' she said slowly, 'what if it's the Lord Mayor himself who is Solomon wotsit. Has anyone considered that?'

'No!' said George decisively. 'It's all too much of a coincidence, after what Henry's told us. Whoever did this wanted Threlfall holed up in this impossible building. It was the one way he could be sure of getting at him with impunity. First he'd scare him into the labyrinth—'

'And then?' interposed Henry.

'And then, *he'd be waiting*.'

Isabelle shivered. 'That's horrible,' she said. 'So

194

cold-blooded.' There was a clatter of steps on the stairs, and Ed and Jane stumbled in, followed by Bruno.

'Here you all are!' said Jane. 'We're dying of boredom upstairs.'

'Bruno,' said George suddenly. 'Where were you at six fifty Monday evening?'

'No idea. Why do you ask?'

'That seems to be the one time the police know where the murderer was. I know where Isabelle, Alasdair and I were, all together, but I don't know about you. So think!'

'I don't need to think,' said Henry. 'I was on stage with all the rest of you when the shot was fired tonight. So it can't have been me.'

'There were two shots,' said George. 'And any one of you could have fired the second, under cover of darkness.'

'I don't think it was Bruno,' put in Jane diffidently. 'He was next to me when the lights went out, and I definitely recognized his hand up my dress!'

'You bastard!' Ed, one eye still oozing blood from his encounter upstairs, made for Bruno. 'She's my wife.' He stopped, struck by a sudden thought. 'Anyway, he's got two hands. What were you doing with the other one, shithead?'

Isabelle was looking abstracted again. 'Alasdair? Where . . . '

Rumbold hurried across to her and took her hands. 'Come on,' he said, smiling. 'While this lot are arguing, you and I could be finding the way in, if Henry'll help us. What are we looking for?'

'A large fireplace,' said Henry. 'Bigger than you'd expect for the size of the room. I'll get my compass . . .'

But Isabelle and Rumbold had already started off back up the stairs.

'You know,' said Bright, listening on headphones to the transmission of this scene via the microphone planted by DS Briggs, 'actors are a race apart, aren't they? It's like a bloody zoo in there.'

Dumeige put down his own headphones and chuckled. 'But Sinclair's right about the Monday night point. I'd like Colonel Lumsden's answer to that question too. He seemed to have some sort of animus against your Lord Mayor.'

'If it'll make you happy, we'll ask everyone. First I want everyone to recheck their statements. Reynolds!'

'Sir.'

'Start with Sinclair and his singers. Get everyone to do their statements again. New piece of paper. Different officer. Then we'll check them again. Then I'm going to let some light into this bloody labyrinth they're talking about, if it exists, that is.'

There was a knock on the door.

'Come!'

'It's the Steward, Mr Edwards,' said Peter anxiously. 'He's not well. But he's demanding to see you.'

'Where is he?' asked Bright angrily. 'In fact I want to have a word with him myself.'

'In his sitting room. On the top floor.'

'You'd better show me the way up then. You coming?'

Dumeige shook his head. 'I think I'll stay here,' he replied.

Chapter Twenty-Six

'Tell me, sir?' Mr Edwards' asthma had taken a distinct turn for the worse and he was lying well back in an old armchair covered in green chintz. 'Is it true the Lord Mayor's been kidnapped?'

'I believe so,' said Bright gravely, and sat down on a chair which creaked. DS Skipwith and DCI Jameson propped themselves against the wall.

'In that case I have something to tell you.' The old man shuddered and passed a hand over his eyes.

'Yes?' Bright gestured frantically to Jameson, who pulled out a small notebook and got ready to take down any statement in shorthand.

'You'll find them perhaps in the passages?' The old man didn't look up.

'Yes,' said Bright, giving Skipwith a significant look. 'You knew about those?'

'It was me who told him about them,' said Mr Edwards. 'Now perhaps I'm thinking I was wrong. But at the time, I thought it could help him get away from this foreign madman.'

'Go on.'

'Well,' Mr Edwards took a deep breath. 'I suppose there's no harm in telling you now.' He was racked by another bout of congested wheezing. 'This . . . asthma . . . ' he choked, 'it'll be the death of me yet.'

Bright had an inspiration and smiled. 'Just take your time, Mr Edwards. Was it you who turned the lights out?'

The old man nodded. 'I hope I wasn't wrong to do that, sir,' he said. 'The Lord Mayor was very insistent. He said it was an idea of his own.'

Bright stared at Jameson. 'The Lord Mayor? You mean Mr Threlfall?'

'Yes, sir. The Lord Mayor it was who told me to turn off the lights. And then count to a hundred.' He wiped his eyes. 'You've no idea how hard it is to count in the dark. I'd got to eighty-six when one of the policemen came along and told me to turn it on again.' He looked as if he might start coughing again.

'I can't believe this,' said Bright, frowning. 'You're really saying it was the *Lord Mayor* who asked you to switch out the main fusebox?'

'Told me, more like,' said Mr Edwards with a slow solemn knowing wink. 'You didn't disregard Mr Threlfall's orders without very good reason. He was the same when he was Sheriff. Four years ago. A very meticulous man. Liked things done just so.'

'Can we get back to these passages,' said Bright,

rubbing the back of his neck again. 'Who else could have known about them?'

Mr Edwards looked around. 'Well, of course, when he was just a lad,' he said. 'It's not really my place, but . . . '

'But?' There was shouting outside. Bright jumped up. 'What—?'

The door burst open. 'We've found her!' DS Briggs came running in. 'We've found her!'

'Who?'

'The tart who visited Solomon in the hotel. They've got her under armed guard at the Gerald Row nick. They're going to fax her photo through now.'

'Let's get down to the office then,' said Bright, a new light in his eyes.

'Yes,' said Skipwith. 'I'm looking forward to seeing Solomon Sinclair's face when he realizes we've found her.'

'You're very sure he's the one.'

'I'm damn certain,' said Skipwith, with some relish. 'Where was he last seen?'

Bright looked at Jameson.

'He was going to check over his statement with DS Reynolds,' said the Chief Inspector. 'He should have been in the office by now. I really don't think—'

'With the fax machine?' shouted Skipwith. *Bloody hell!*' He began to run down the stairs.

*

In the security office, George stood up to stretch his legs after another exhaustive check and double-check of his earlier statement.

'I wish I could tell you more,' he said, and the Sergeant grinned.

'I wish you could too, sir,' he replied. A bell rang momentarily and one of the machines on the central console began to vibrate. 'Hello!' he said. 'Fax coming. Like some more tea in a minute?'

'I'd love some,' said George with genuine fervour. 'I can't think of anything I'd like more.'

A thin pellucid strip of paper began, very slowly, to creep across the desk, discharged, as it seemed, from the groaning machine like the immaculate motion of some mechanical bowel.

As he watched, fascinated, a face appeared, a greyish indistinct image, starting with the neck and widening out to show the chin, the wide mouth, the nose and cheeks—

'Hello!' said George. 'I know that girl.'

'I thought you might,' said Skipwith triumphantly from the doorway, his face scarlet with exhaustion but the gun in his hand was held perfectly straight. 'George Tassilo Sinclair, I arrest you . . . '

'Hold on, Sergeant,' snapped Bright, appearing behind him. 'Perhaps you'd be kind enough to allow me to deal with this, since we're in the City of London?'

Skipwith had to hold himself in, to turn away

with the deference necessary to a senior officer, but his eyes were half-squinting from the effort, and he let out a thin whistling breath of air.

'I'm sorry, sir,' he said. 'He's admitted—'

'There's no admitting!' blurted George. 'I know this girl. How does she come into it?'

'Sit down,' said Bright calmly. 'Reynolds!'

'Sir!'

'Oblige me by fetching the tape recorder from next door. We want to do this properly.'

'Would you like a nice cup of tea, Mr Sinclair?' enquired Skipwith, anxious to rehabilitate himself but earning only a scowl from the Commander.

'Actually,' said George, 'I would. In fact, we were only saying—'

'Make it five,' snapped Bright. 'Now,' he said, when the paraphernalia was all in place, and George had been duly cautioned and supplied with a large cup of strong sweet tea the colour of iron ore. 'What can you tell us about this lady?'

'That's easy,' said George. 'She was at a nightclub I went to. The Dancing Dervish.' He stared at the photostat. 'She's much prettier in real life.'

'Have you slept with her?' asked Skipwith casually through gritted teeth.

George shook his head. 'She did suggest it,' he said. 'But she said she was expensive, and anyway . . . '

'And anyway . . . ?' prompted Bright.

'Anyway I've been too busy,' said George with happy inspiration.

'But you met her again at the hotel?' said Bright, feigning confusion.

'Hotel?'

'Yes. The Black Friar.'

George frowned. 'I've never heard of it.'

'She remembers you,' put in Jameson. 'And the manager has positively identified your photograph.'

'You probably shouldn't have paid him in cash,' chuckled Bright. 'That's why he remembers you so well!'

'In cash?'

Bright nodded. 'Your only mistake,' he said. 'Otherwise it's been brilliant. An education for all of us.'

'Forensic picked up your DNA from a swab,' murmured Jameson. 'They were *very* impressed with your thoroughness too.'

George stared at them. 'They were?'

'Oh yes,' said Bright, his eyes gleaming now. 'We all think you're a genius!'

'I'm glad to hear it,' said George. 'But the only time I met this girl was at this nightclub. She works there.'

For half an hour they persisted, but George was unshakeable on his sole connection with the girl.

Bright, conscious that if this was the truth

then the murderer was still upstairs, tried a different tack.

'Tell me,' he said, 'if the girl knew anyone else at the nightclub?'

George shook his head. 'Who is she anyway?'

'She is,' said Bright heavily, 'the only person we know to have met Solomon and lived!'

George stared. 'She met the maniac?'

'In a hotel near here. She also works for an escort agency.'

'She *slept* with him?'

'She'll certainly be able to identify him.' Bright turned to Jameson. 'It was the manager who made some reference to them messing up the room, wasn't it?'

'Reference,' said George suddenly. '*Reference!* My God!' He stood up, causing Jameson and Skipwith to tense themselves in case he tried to run.

'You've got to let me talk to her!'

'All in good time,' said Bright. 'She's on her way over here now.' He smiled at George, the forced tricky smile of the cat just a paw's length from a particularly stupid mouse. 'But tell me why you're so keen to talk to her.'

'Because,' said George, 'I've just remembered something.'

'Yes, George? I may call you George, may I?'

'Please do,' said George distractedly. '*Reference.* She said something. It may be important.'

DS Briggs hurried in. 'She's here, sir.'

'Bring her in.'

George stood up as the girl from the nightclub, her face taut with fear, was led in by a stocky police-woman wearing a gun.

'Do you recognize this man?' demanded Bright.

'Yes,' she said, giving George an encouraging smile as she sat down in Commander Bright's chair.

'From the hotel?'

She frowned. 'The hotel? No, this is my friend I met at The Dancing Dervish.'

'This is so important,' broke in George, ignoring Bright's exclamation. Dumeige had walked in, with Gerard who was still wearing his police badge clipped to his tailcoat. 'When you saw me in the nightclub . . . '

'Mmm?'

'You said something about a reference.'

'This is the wrong scene for that kind of talk, honey.' She giggled irrepressibly.

George fixed her with a serious stare. 'You knew someone, didn't you?'

'Know a lot of people,' she mumbled.

'Did you know anyone I was with?'

She stopped and sat up. 'Yes!' she said, her eyes round. 'The tall man Smith. He was the man at the hotel. And I'd say he was dangerous from what I saw of him. Which was mostly from underneath!'

'Tabley? Where did you come across him?'

'Some hotel in the City. He wanted . . . ' She shrugged her slender shoulders. 'Everyone wants something odd. Look at you. You only brought me here because you wanted to find out about your friend.'

'He's not my friend. He's a murderer. Someone's got to stop him. You called him Smith? Why do you think that's his name?'

'Because,' she said, 'he's got an account.'

'You've got him!' said George looking round triumphantly. 'Lord Snooty Tabley. Who'd have thought a toff like that would be a fucking *lunatic*?' Bright was shouting instructions over a microphone, and George was startled to see Gerard, still dressed as *Alfredo*, pulling another snub-nosed revolver out of his trousers.

'Good,' said the girl, trying to recapture his attention. 'But be careful. He was really weird with me. The worst thing was he's got these thick tufts of hair on his back. He made me . . . '

George, staring, interrupted her, 'But you said the *tall* man!'

'You're tall to me,' she said, lowering her eyelids and running a tentative finger across his chest. 'I meant the man who was buying the drinks, not the fucking giant.'

'Oh my God! Isabelle's gone with him.'

'And who's she?' asked the girl sharply, but he was already moving towards where Bright, white-faced, had answered the telephone and was listening to whatever was being said. He handed the receiver to George. 'It's your sister,' he said. 'She wants a word.'

Chapter Twenty-Seven

'Isabelle!'

'What?'

'Why does your voice sound funny?'

'Well,' she said. 'It might be because I've strained it singing *Violetta*. But actually it's because Alasdair's holding a very sharp knife under my chin.'

George took a deep breath. 'I see.'

'I'm glad you do,' she said, 'because the view this end is pretty ropey.'

'Can I speak to him?'

'I wouldn't.'

'Why not?'

'He's in a funny mood. Aren't you, *chéri*?' The line went suddenly dead.

'Where the hell's he ringing from?' shouted Bright.

'Mobile,' said the man by the switchboard. 'I'll give you the number directly.'

'He's up in those passages,' said George. 'Let me go in after him. The entrance is by some fireplace.'

'Fireplace!' shouted Bright. 'On the landing! Where the shot came from. Have they moved the old woman's body yet?' Skipwith, his face dark with disappointment, nodded. 'Right! Let's get in there.'

'Please,' said George. 'Let me come.'

'This is a police job,' said Jameson repressively. 'Leave him to us.'

'She's my sister,' said George. 'And I'm responsible for her.' And before anyone thought to stop him, he had ducked under DS Reynolds' restraining arm and was racing up the oak staircase.

He was still fumbling in the fireplace where he had found that the fireback was on some kind of hinge when Bright, wearing a flak-jacket, and carrying what looked like a small machine-gun, pushed him aside and a uniformed man with a crowbar squeezed under the carved marble chimney-piece.

'Can't you understand plain English?' Bright snapped angrily. 'Leave this to us. I've got officers going in from all over. There won't be a fucking fireplace in the whole building by the time I've finished. You stay here with Briggs.' There was a creak from the fireback, and the other officer, his face black with soot, backed out of the hole. Bright ducked his head under the mantelpiece and disappeared through the narrow gap.

'Are *you* Briggs?' asked George in a puzzled voice.

'Yes, sir,' said the officer stolidly.

'Then who's that?' asked George, and hit the man on the side of his head when he turned. Quickly he squeezed through a grimy slit revealed by the fire-back and, even then, cunningly placed at the very corner of the recess. Immediately he was faced with stairs, tiny, narrow, winding stairs that corkscrewed away down into blackness.

'It's like being in a coffin!' said Bright ahead of him. It was true. The walls were lined with panels of the thinnest finest oak, untouched over nearly three centuries.

The smell, too, was of graveyards, heavy, musty odours came and went, as dry cobwebs brushed against his face and twice he nearly lost his footing. Now they were climbing at an angle, with each single footing rising alternately like a crow-stepped gable.

'Is that you, Jameson?' called back Bright, the flash of his torch momentarily lighting the basic geometry of the winding stairs.

'It's me,' called George. 'George Sinclair,' and heard the policeman gasp. 'I'm here to help my sister,' he said. 'I'm no murderer.' The torchlight had gone out, and he felt giddy and vulnerable on that steep and insubstantial stairway.

'Come up here with your hands where I can see them,' said Bright.

He stumbled on up. 'I'm doing my best!' The torch suddenly blazed up again, half-blinding him.

'I told you to stay out,' said Bright angrily.

George shrugged. 'Imagine being in here, with all those soldiers searching for you. It must have been terrifying,' he whispered. 'I think there's someone behind us.'

'There should be,' said Bright. 'I've got half the City force in here by now.' There was the flash of more torches and Jameson and Dumeige, the latter holding a small automatic, came out of a separate stairway, coughing in a cloud of dust and soot.

'The boffin says watch out for loose boards,' hissed Jameson. 'He says there may be false floor-boards above sheer drops within the walls, thirty, forty feet deep. Fucking mantraps.'

'Now he tells us!' said Bright. Twice they heard voices very near, and once the bark of a dog and the sound of it scratching, right against the thin oak boards. On they crept, sweeping the walls ahead with their torches, coughing in the dank fetid air.

Suddenly the narrow passage curved and they came to an arch with a narrow wooden door, half open.

'Shall I kick it?' asked Jameson.

'It won't need that,' said George, and pushed gently on the ancient timber.

It creaked dreadfully, but Bright walked through and shone his torch round what seemed quite a sizeable chamber after what they'd been through, perhaps three metres square. It was all George could do to choke down a scream that rose in his throat. For opposite, watching them in silence, was a seated figure, apparently draped in lace, and *grinning* at them in the dim half-light.

'Who in God's name is that?' Jameson shone his torch full on the figure, revealing that what they had thought was lace was, in fact, fine cobwebs and where first impressions showed a face, a second glance revealed just the fleshless bone and eyeless sockets of a skull. They were looking at a skeleton, but a skeleton draped in full eighteenth-century regalia.

'I believe,' said George, his spine tingling with fear and fascination, 'that we are in the august presence of the late Sir Wilbraham Smith, Lord Mayor of London.'

Chapter Twenty-Eight

'Sir Who?' said Bright. 'What about Threlfall . . . '

'Sir Wilbraham,' said George, still gazing fixedly at the polished skull gaping blankly at them from its ragged shroud of red satin, 'was Lord Mayor of London in 1745. Mr Edwards told me about him and didn't you hear what my baritone was telling us about him downstairs. He disappeared too. He must have starved to death in here, rather than face being hung, drawn and quartered.'

Bright stared at him suspiciously. 'So you knew about this passage all the time?'

George shook his head. 'Of course not. Though I think Mr Edwards must have. Or at least deduced its existence. He said people'd have been surprised if the house had been bombed. I couldn't think what he meant. Now I understand.'

Jameson shook his head in disbelief. 'Two hundred and fifty years! You'd think they'd have smelt him.'

'Come on,' said Bright. 'We're supposed to be looking for Threlfall and your sister.'

'*Commandeur!*' called Dumeige, who had moved away from the group during the explanation. 'There's a bigger room through here!' He went through and let out an inarticulate cry.

The others crowded through after him. There, at the end of another weird little passage, was a tall chamber, its vaulted ceiling a modest echo of the great hall in whose ceiling this space had been concealed.

And there too, facing them, bolt upright in a second silver throne, in grotesque parody of that other skeleton, sat Threlfall, the missing Lord Mayor. There was his crisp scarlet robe, though torn in a couple of places, and there his large red ham-like hands, wired to the arms of the chair. But where his face had been there was now nothing but a ragged blood-soaked mass of splintered bone, and his white lace cravat was caked an ugly reddish-black.

'*Christ!*' George had one hand over his mouth. Jameson had bent over and was vomiting in the corner. Dumeige just stood there, his mouth hanging open. 'What happened?'

'Shot through the back of the head,' mumbled Dumeige, wiping his mouth on the back of his sleeve, 'with a soft-nosed bullet. It expands, you see,' he added unnecessarily. 'You'll find his face over there.' None of them looked.

'What's that doing here?' demanded Bright.

Beside the dead man was placed a small plate. On it was a half-eaten croissant and a piece of fruit cake, the pathetic remains of the Lord Mayor's breakfast.

Somewhere close, someone *laughed*.

Immediately all the torches were extinguished. 'Try to the right,' whispered Bright to someone, probably Dumeige, and at the same time George felt someone edge past him. He held himself very still, and listened for what seemed an age. He could hear shuffling, a distant creak and then, far off, there was the sound of a shot. Instinctively he crouched, and then gasped aloud as a sudden crash overhead was followed by a shocking intrusion of light. Someone, a uniformed policeman, had fallen through the sloping wall of the chamber and was lying, winded, on the floor. Behind him, the wall was revealed as part of the cove of the Egyptian Hall through which poured the light of a thousand bulbs.

'Jesus Christ!' moaned the policeman, his back arching with the pain. 'I've broke my fucking leg.'

Jameson knelt down to help him, and George slipped quickly down the passageway where the shot had come from. He was almost immediately in total darkness again, and he shuffled forwards as quickly as he dared. False floorboards! What sadistic bastards they'd been in those days. Far in front he saw the gleam of a torch ahead. It was Bright. The policeman was hurrying forward. Suddenly there was a loud creak and a strange, accelerating, cry of fear. Bright had completely disappeared.

'Oh *dear*,' said a voice in the darkness. 'I believe the Commander has just fallen fifty-seven feet on to good marble. That won't be a pretty sight.'

George held himself very still.

'I know you're there,' said the voice. 'I think that's my friend, George Sinclair, isn't it?' A shaft of light blazed in his face. After a moment, he could make out three figures, only about twenty feet away from him.

'Put it down,' said George. 'There's no need to hurt Isabelle. Not now.' Now that his eyes were growing used to the light, he could see that her dress was dreadfully torn and stained. 'Why you—!'

'Don't!' croaked Isabelle. 'What does it matter?'

'I'm tired,' said Rumbold. 'It was fun to start with, but now I'm tired.'

'I don't understand,' said George, frantic now to maintain a conversation. He could hear the sound of sawing in the distance, and other muffled sounds of policemen entering the passages.

'I'll tell you,' said Isabelle, her *Violetta* wig very askew, holding her chin very high because of the knife. 'Because Alasdair was telling me about it while he . . . ' She was having difficulty talking. 'Alasdair's father was driven to suicide by some swindle or other.' In front of them, eyes open, staring up at the ceiling, lay the dead body of Paul Dumeige.

'I *explained*, you bitch! I told you everything.' Rumbold's voice was grainy now, like an old long-playing record.

'I know,' she gasped, feeling the prick of the knife. 'I just can't take it all in. George, darling?'

'Yes?' He forced himself to sound normal, relaxed. Somewhere, quite close, a dog whimpered.

'Why did you say you knew where Alasdair was Monday night?'

'Because he came to collect you for the opera. He tooted his horn.'

'I thought that's why,' she said. 'Actually that was his driver, Stefan. He saw me looking at him after you'd said that. That's why he brought me up here.'

'Sorry,' said George. 'But it wouldn't have made any difference, Alasdair. They've got the girl you were with in the hotel downstairs. There's no point any more.'

There was a long silence, broken only by more sawing in the rafters somewhere above them, and then Rumbold sighed. 'I'm so tired,' he whispered again. 'So tired.' A cloud of fine dust came blowing past him. Everywhere light was being let into the labyrinth, as men with dogs and crowbars forced their way in.

'I understand . . . sort of . . . about the four businessmen,' said Isabelle, desperate to keep his attention. 'But why shoot that poor old woman?'

'What poor old woman?' There was spittle on his lips now.

'Dorothy, the maid.'

'I didn't shoot her,' sighed Rumbold. 'Reggie must have shot her because she saw him entering the passages through the chimney. He'd already killed Gooch, so he was past caring.'

'*Killed Gooch?*'

'Well, you don't think I did that, do you?' He laughed, a strange sound. 'Why would I want to kill poor old Dick Gooch? I was sitting next to you when it happened. Gave me the fright of my life, the lights going off like that. That was down to Reggie. Had to be. I expect Gooch had found out about Reggie's frauds, and being an officer and a gentleman, he'd gone and told Reggie. Old Reg must have seen my presence as the perfect cover. Last throw of a desperate man.' His voice was ebbing and cracking. It was, thought George, as if he had climbed some great mountain, and was now dragging himself wearily back to base camp.

'But you must have fired that shot that ended up in Threlfall's chair.'

Rumbold nodded. 'At the time it seemed too good a chance to miss. Actually it was a foolish risk, because if I had hit him, they'd have tried to search everyone in the room and I'd have had some little difficulty getting away.' Eddies of sound, hushed whispers, the scuffing of a shoe echoed softly in the darkness round them.

'You might have killed anyone in the dark.'

'I know,' said Rumbold with something of a return of his former spirit. 'It would have kept me awake for *weeks* worrying about it. Those people go out and maybe kill a hundred, a *thousand* pheasants in an afternoon. I'm not saying that's the same, but it makes you think, doesn't it? Anyway, he got away, and I got back to my seat for our little keyboard relationship. I knew even then I would be killing you soon. It added *zest* to our partnership.' He chuckled. 'Well, I thought so, anyway.' Help was close at hand now. George could hear whispering behind him, and behind Rumbold too.

'You always knew about these passages?' asked George. 'That was very clever of you.'

'No, it wasn't,' snarled Rumbold. 'I was brought up in this building.'

'*Really?*' George stared.

'Yes!' He chuckled. 'My father was Lord Mayor. I was a child when old Edwards first told me about them. Of course I made it my business to find them after that. And here he is, the doddering old fart, still messing about as Steward. He's been alive twenty years longer than my father. *My father!*' There were tears running down his cheeks, dribbling off his chin, yet the knife under Isabelle's chin never wavered.

'You told me your father was in a very nice private home,' croaked Isabelle reproachfully.

'*Stepfather*, bitch,' snarled Rumbold. 'How could I inherit the baronetcy if my father was still alive, eh? That's my stepfather, but he was good to me, and I've been good to him. He had everything my father lost. He had my mother, anytime he wanted her. He had me as a ready-made son.' He wiped his chin impatiently. 'But he was good to me.'

'Took you a bit of time,' said George, casually leaning against the wooden wall of the passage, and wondering what was delaying the cavalry. They must be waiting for someone to give the order.

'What did?'

'Getting round to dealing with these bods. What held you up?'

'What held me *up*?' His voice had sunk again to a whisper. 'I didn't *know*. Why my Daddy did it. Why he left me alone. I didn't fucking *understand*! Until I started reviewing the evidence on a case I was prosecuting for the Serious Fraud Squad. Once I saw the evidence, not enough to prosecute . . . I had to advise them that myself . . . but enough to tell *me.*' He nodded triumphantly. 'Oh *yes*! I knew all right. I'm no fool.'

'I can see *that*,' said George.

'You smarmy bastard. Hold on, please!' He

pushed Isabelle aside and slackened his grip on her in order to draw the long gun with its unwieldy silencer. 'Take this!' He aimed the gun straight at George and then screamed, screamed so shrilly that George ran forward at the gun regardless, thinking that Rumbold had hurt Isabelle. It was the other way round. Isabelle had thrust Jane's long hatpin straight through his right eye and into his brain.

Solomon, though still standing, his body wedged against the narrow wall, was clinically dead.

Chapter Twenty-Nine

'Bye then!' Bruno, shouldering his black suede bag, was on his way out. The tumults and the shoutings had died away, and the Inspectors and the Chief Inspectors were all departed. Another day, another show. Baritones are *famous* for their relaxed outlook on life.

Not like tenors. Rupert was still sitting in the corner of the ornate dressing room, crouched rather, his eyes glazed and his lips quivering, just enough to show.

'Here's your travel money!' said George brusquely.

Rupert looked up. 'What travel money?' The whole concept was totally alien to the Floria Tosca Company's ethos.

George shrugged. 'Lady Tabley gave it to me, a fiver each. Don't feel you've got to . . . ' but the note had already been snatched from his hand and secreted somewhere in Rupert's voluminous leathers.

'George.'

'Yes, Rupert?'

'Never, *ever*, ask me to do another opera for you, *please.*'

'What's this?' Isabelle, her pale face gleaming with some freshly applied make-up, came up and slipped her arm through George's.

'Rupert doesn't want to work with us again.' The tenor now had two fingers placed against his unsteady mouth.

'Rupes, *darling*!' She bent over and stroked his cheek satirically. 'You were so brave.'

Rupert bridled at the sarcasm. 'I'm sorry,' he snapped. 'Tonight was *too much.*'

'Well, at least you didn't get blood all over your corsage like me,' she retorted. 'You try sticking a hatpin into someone's eye! It's no joke . . . '

'Isabelle! *Puleeze!*'

One by one, the singers packed up their meagre belongings and gave their costumes to Jane. Baron or Marquis just for an hour or two, they handed back the tiaras, the gold studs, the *Légion d'Honneurs* of their brief eminence and resumed the quiet humdrum identity of young singers struggling for a living, or, better still, recognition in one of Europe's capital cities.

Swapping tailcoats for anoraks, a silk ballgown

for a nylon jersey, their personalities underwent a similar change, from larger to smaller than life, or so it seemed to Peter and Dennis the footmen watching from the further doorway, waiting for their chance to tidy the room before retiring to bed.

'Uh, George?' It was Rupert, back again to retrieve a glove.

'Rupert?'

'I didn't mean it.'

George stared. 'Mean what?'

'That I wouldn't take another job.' He chuckled uneasily. 'You know me. I'm anybody's for a square meal!'

George clapped him on the back. 'Great!' he said, feigning delight. 'We'll be in touch . . . soon, I hope.'

Outside in the lobby, the big maid was hoovering the carpet, her face very red and her eyes smudged with make-up that had run. There were also a couple of uniformed policemen sitting, apparently exhausted, on one of the wide blue and gold settees with their shoes undone and he caught a glimpse of Brigadier Popham in the distance, unexpectedly dapper in a pale blue paisley dressing gown. George hurried through and down the stairs into the entrance hall.

'You'd best go out the other way,' said the Porter in a weary voice that smelt of gin. 'It's bloody bedlam out there. Television, the works!' He looked very unsteady on his feet, and there was just a touch of stubble showing, caught by the strangely garish light pouring through the opaque windows.

George shook his head, too tired to worry. 'They won't bother me,' he said. Opera impresarios, like plumbers, grow used to a sharp change in the social climate before and after performances. Before, they are an essential source of reassurance for the panic-stricken hostess, and as such are fed on a rich mixture of flattery and respect. After, they are abruptly changed into just another unnecessary encumbrance, and, what's more, one that doesn't seem to know when to leave!

As soon as the old Porter pulled back the heavy bolts, released the chain and opened the door, the source of the strange light was explained. The whole street was blazing with arc-lights. It was as if Walbrook and the west front of the Mansion House had become the stage of La Scala for one night. There were the crowds, the *chorus*. He half expected an orchestra to add to the din.

But he was right about the Press taking no notice of him, an untidy man in a dusty suit, shortish, tired and dressed to blend into the crowd of a thousand other mediocrities. For there, in the middle, a rich blaze of exultant red, bathed in love by the cameras, stood Maria, head high, jowl tucked in, breasts thrust out, the very model of the genus *diva splendens*.

' . . . yes,' she was saying, 'there was blood, **blood**, darlings, **everywhere**, but I kept the note. It was

225

what I *had* to do, you understand, it is how we are trained, in Grand Opera. As *Maestro* Muti always tells me: "Maria, your *rrrruns* make Sutherland sound like a tired old tram . . . " '

George smiled, and slipped quietly away into the night.